PRETTY IN PINK

HOUSEMATES #6

JAY NORTHCOTE

*To Lindsay
love
Jay Northcote
x*

Cover artist: Garrett Leigh.
Editor: Victoria Milne.
Pretty in Pink © 2018 Jay Northcote.

ALL RIGHTS RESERVED

This literary work may not be reproduced or transmitted in any form or by any means, including electronic or photographic reproduction, in whole or in part, without express written permission.
This is a work of fiction and any resemblance to persons, living or dead, or business establishments, events or locales is coincidental.
The Licensed Art Material is being used for illustrative purposes only.
All Rights Are Reserved. No part of this may be used or reproduced in any manner whatsoever without written permission, except in the case of brief quotations embodied in critical articles and reviews.

Warning

This book contains material that is intended for a mature, adult audience. It contains graphic language, explicit sexual content, and adult situations.

ONE

February

RYAN WAS a few drinks down and feeling pretty buzzed when he first caught sight of blond hair through the crowd of partygoers.

He nearly hadn't bothered coming out tonight. He had his third year project to write up, and should have been working on that, not partying with his next door neighbours. But the rest of Ryan's housemates had talked him into it and he could do with letting off some steam, so he hadn't put up much of a fight. One night couldn't make too much difference, right?

The blonde arrived late and headed straight into the throng of dancers in the living room, bottle in hand. Tall and leggy in black skinny jeans with shit-kicking boots, Ryan's interest was piqued immediately and a spike of arousal made his cock wake up. Tall and blonde was completely Ryan's type, but when this blond slid a leather jacket off slender shoulders and tossed it on the back of the sofa, his washboard-flat chest made it clear he was a guy—so not Ryan's type after all.

Despite the gut punch of disappointment at that revelation, Ryan found his interest persisted. The guy drew Ryan's attention like a magnet lining up iron filings, and no matter how hard he tried, Ryan couldn't stop watching him.

Spurred on by alcohol and reckless impulsivity, Ryan made a conscious decision not to question his attraction and just roll with it. He gradually edged his way into the group where the blond was dancing, and when he finally managed to make eye contact, the guy gave him a knowing smile that reflected Ryan's interest right back at him. It curled around Ryan's balls like the gentle, insistent squeeze of a hand.

Game on.

University was supposed to be all about new experiences, and Ryan only had a few months left before he graduated. He'd never hooked up with a guy before, and it had always been on his sexual bucket list, but not a high priority. As a young teen he'd sometimes admired androgynous male models on the pages of magazines that his mum used to buy and felt a confusing interest in them... but he'd never seen a guy in real life he'd wanted to fuck enough to actually do something about it.

Until tonight.

The guy moved closer to Ryan, his pale hair falling over one eye as he circled his hips suggestively in time to the heavy beat of the dance music that blared out of the speakers. He offered the bottle in his hand to Ryan. Not bothering to look at the label, Ryan took it and kept his eyes fixed on the blond as he wrapped his lips around the neck and tilted it to take a huge gulp. Sweet, fruity, fizzy stuff trickled over his tongue and made him choke in surprise. Coughing, he wiped the back of his mouth. "What the fuck is this?" he yelled over the music.

The blond said something he couldn't catch, so Ryan moved closer, cupping his hand up to his ear. "Prosecco and peach schnapps. It's like Bellini, only with an extra kick." Warm breath tickled Ryan's skin, leaving a tingling desire for contact.

Ryan took another more cautious swallow before handing it back. The taste of alcohol was strong after the beer Ryan had been drinking earlier. "Thanks."

"You're welcome." The guy grinned.

Wanting to maintain their connection, Ryan leaned in to speak into his ear. "I'm Ryan, by the way. What's your name?"

"Johnny. It's nice to meet you, Ryan." Switching the bottle to his left hand, Johnny offered his right hand to Ryan, who took it, and shook, charmed by the unusually formal greeting. Johnny's hand was slender, but he had a strong grip that made Ryan imagine how it might feel wrapped around another part of his anatomy as Johnny maintained the contact for a beat longer than was usual.

They went back to dancing.

Ryan knew he wasn't a great dancer. Normally he didn't care if he looked a bit daft on the dance floor, but with Johnny's gaze on him he suddenly felt as though he had two left feet and didn't know what to do with his arms. Johnny, on the other hand, moved with a rhythmic, sinuous grace that made Ryan long to see his supple body with fewer clothes on.

Hoping to restart the conversation, Ryan moved close again. "So, how do you know these guys?" he said loudly in

Johnny's ear, waving his hand vaguely around the crowded room. "Are you a friend of Ben's?" This was Ben's birthday party, so he was the most likely connection.

Johnny's lips moved, but his reply was lost in the thump of the bass.

"What?" Ryan leaned closer still.

Warm breath on Ryan's ear made him shiver as Johnny said, "It's too loud in here to have a conversation. You wanna talk instead of dance?"

Ryan drew back to see Johnny's eyebrows raised in question. He nodded and mouthed, "Yeah," with a shrug that was supposed to be nonchalant, but he wasn't quite sure he pulled it off.

Johnny grinned and jerked his head in a clear signal to follow, so Ryan did, staying close as Johnny wove his way through the dancing people and out into the hallway. It was bright out there, and Ryan took the opportunity to admire Johnny's legs again. Long and slim in black jeans that looked as though they'd been painted on, they led up to a tight little arse that was less curvy than the ones Ryan usually noticed. He reckoned those cheeks would fit perfectly in his palms, and found the thought rather appealing. Ryan had always been an arse man. Honestly, he could take or leave tits, but a nice arse always got his attention and Johnny's was in his sights.

Johnny sat on the bottom of the stairs and patted the step beside him, so Ryan joined him.

"That's better." Johnny smiled, warm and genuine. "Much quieter out here." He took a sip from his bottle, and then handed it to Ryan.

Ryan lifted it to his lips, achingly aware that Johnny's mouth had just been right there as he took a mouthful.

When he lowered the bottle, Johnny was watching him. His eyes were striking, more grey than blue, and there was black eyeliner smudged around them, making them stand out in Johnny's pale face. He was insanely pretty. No wonder Ryan had thought he was a girl at first. He looked like he'd stepped out of one of those fashion magazines that Ryan used to sneak up to his room to study more closely when he was a teenager. At first he'd been interested in the photos of the women, but sometimes the feminine-looking men caught his attention too.

Suddenly a memory emerged vividly.

There was one particular set of pictures he'd been obsessed by: a blond male model with long hair like Johnny's, his flat chest clearly visible in a fur gilet that hung open over pale skin and pink nipples. In one photo the guy had been shirtless in black leather trousers and heavy black boots—much like the ones Johnny was wearing now. In another, his pert little arse was turned towards the camera as he looked over his shoulder in a sultry, teasing pose. Ryan had been around fourteen or fifteen at the time, and he'd only jerked off to pictures of girls before, or porn he managed to find online. But something about that model pushed all his buttons. He'd torn the photos out of the magazine and hidden them inside an atlas in his bedroom. Then he'd jerked off over them several nights a week for a few months, feeling weird about it—because he didn't think he was gay—but unable to resist the urge to look at them. Ryan had imagined running his hands over that leather-clad arse and squeezing, rubbing his cock against it. He'd imagined the guy jerking off with Ryan kneeling over him, until they both came all over that flat chest and stomach. It had been a regular fantasy until Ryan got his first girlfriend and discovered the joys of getting his dick sucked, and being able to squeeze a real arse instead of drooling over a photo of one. Then he'd forgotten about the photos, and he wondered what had ever happened to them. They'd probably ended up going to the charity shop with the atlas when he cleared out some stuff a few years later.

"You look like you've seen a ghost," Johnny drawled, amusement painted on his features.

Ryan realised he was staring like an idiot, and a hot blush crawled up from under his collar to heat his face. "Sorry," he muttered. "You just remind me of uh... someone I used to know."

Johnny's grin widened, and of course he couldn't possibly know what Ryan had been thinking, but Ryan's cheeks burned hotter anyway. He changed the subject quickly. "So, I tried to ask before. How do you know Ben?"

"His boyfriend, Sid, is my flatmate." Johnny reached for the bottle in Ryan's hand, his warm fingers brushing Ryan's as he took it. Ryan watched helplessly as Johnny swallowed, fascinated by the bob of his throat and the way he licked his lips afterwards. He felt dizzy, probably partly from the alcohol, but it was more than that. Johnny made him disorientated, clumsy, and nervous. It was like being an awkward teenager all over again.

Johnny shuffled a little closer until their knees were touching. "So how do *you* know Ben?"

"I live in the house next door."

"Are you a student then?" Johnny asked.

"Yeah."

An awkward pause.

"What are you studying?" Johnny was patient. Ryan seemed to have forgotten the art of conversation. All his usual chatty confidence had deserted him. He wanted desperately to impress, but was fucking this up badly. Johnny must think he was a right tit.

"Chemistry." Ryan gave a nervous chuckle. "It's not very exciting."

"Should get you a decent job though, right?" Johnny said. "At least you won't end up working in retail like me. Half the people working with me are graduates, some even have PhDs. It's ridiculous." He sounded nonchalant, but the frown that marred his brow contradicted his light tone.

"Yeah. The job market is tough. Where do you work?"

"Top Man," Johnny said. "It's boring, but it pays the bills. And at least I get a staff discount." He stroked the legs of his black skinny jeans. "I just got these yesterday because my old ones were ripped."

"They look good on you," Ryan blurted.

Johnny turned his grey gaze on him and his lips curved in a sexy smile. "Yeah?" Ryan nodded dumbly. "Thanks. I think they show off my assets. That's why I chose them."

"They definitely do," Ryan managed.

"Want more of this?" Johnny offered the bottle and Ryan took it again. He sipped, not sure he needed much more alcohol to dull his wits.

"Thanks. It's a bit sweet for me." Ryan wrinkled his nose, but kept hold of the bottle as Johnny made no move to take it back.

"You sweet enough already?" Johnny grinned at his own cheesy joke.

Ryan chuckled. "Something like that."

"So what do you usually drink? No... let me guess. Beer?"

"Yeah. Am I that predictable?"

"You look the type." Johnny let his cool grey gaze rake assessingly over Ryan.

"Is that a bad thing?"

"Nah. I have a thing for masc guys who are into beer and cars and hammering things really hard." He smirked, and Ryan was glad he didn't have a mouthful of drink otherwise he'd probably have choked again. *Fuck*. His dick was getting hard at the images that had conjured up. He was still scrambling for a good response when he was saved by the arrival of Ben and Sid coming around the corner from the direction of the living room. Ben was holding onto Sid's arm and they looked flushed and giddy. With Sid's crotch at their eye level, the telltale bulge was obvious.

"Well, this looks cosy," Sid said. "Excuse us."

Ryan felt his cheeks burn again as he stood to let them through, wondering what they made of him and Johnny nose-to-nose on the stairs. Johnny stayed sitting where he was with a shit-eating grin on his face. "Have fun, kids, and don't forget to use lots of lube."

Sid flipped up his middle finger at Johnny.

Ben replied, "Oh, don't worry. We never skimp." He met Johnny's gaze, and Ryan admired his confidence in dealing with Johnny's teasing.

Johnny smirked. "Good man." Then he looked up at Ryan, who was feeling even more hot and bothered after their exchange. "Lube always beats spit if you're on the receiving end." He licked his lips and let his gaze slide down to Ryan's crotch. Ryan's cock tingled, thickening, and filling. He wondered whether Johnny could tell what he was doing to him.

Ben took Sid's hand, and they squeezed past Johnny and headed upstairs.

Ryan sat back down gratefully, leaning forward to hide his erection, and wishing he could adjust himself but not wanting to make his arousal obvious.

When they were gone, Johnny laughed. "Ben's really come out of his shell. He was so awkward when he first started seeing Sid. Now I can hardly get a rise out of him." He put a hand on Ryan's knee and took the bottle again. The way he licked his lips and parted them slowly should be illegal, Ryan couldn't look away. Johnny's palm was warm through his jeans and he slid it up Ryan's thigh as he took a long, slow swallow. Ryan's cock jerked, painfully hard now with Johnny's fingertips just a few inches away.

When he was done drinking, Johnny patted Ryan's thigh. "Is this okay? I think you're into me. Am I reading this right?"

"Yeah." Ryan's voice came out a hoarse croak. He cleared his throat and tried again. "Yeah. I'm into you. But I've never...." He swallowed and lowered his voice even though there was nobody else around. "I've never hooked up with a guy before."

Johnny's face lit up and his eyes gleamed. "Yeah? And do you wanna hook up with me?"

This was it. The moment of truth. Even through the haze of arousal and alcohol Ryan knew that whatever happened, this would always be one of those crossroads in his life where he'd look back and see that the decision he'd made had been an important one.

It didn't take him long to choose his path. He wanted Johnny, and he was curious to know what it would be like with a guy. Even if he decided it wasn't for him he wouldn't regret experimenting.

"Yes."

He was rewarded with another dose of Johnny's sexy smile as Johnny slid his hand right up to the final destination, grabbing Ryan's cock and squeezing, making Ryan gasp. "Wanna take this back to your place then? I'm guessing you'd rather I didn't blow you on the stairs, and it'll be quieter at yours."

"Okay. Yeah." Ryan stood and Johnny's hand fell away from his crotch. He adjusted his dick, and checked his pocket for his keys. "Let's go." He led the way, trusting that Johnny would follow.

TWO

The cold February air shocked Johnny's senses as they stepped out into the darkness. He'd left his leather jacket in the living room, but he wasn't going to break the mood and go back for it now. Ryan was a wet dream come true, but he was nervous. While Johnny was all about consent, he didn't want to give Ryan time to panic and back out. Straight—or straightish—boys were like highly strung racehorses, prone to bolting if you didn't keep them on a tight rein.

The sooner he got his mouth on Ryan's cock the better, because Johnny prided himself on his dick-sucking skills. Once he was working Ryan over with his lips and tongue, Ryan wouldn't have the headspace left to overthink things and freak out.

He followed Ryan down the short path and then up to the neighbouring front door. As Ryan got his keys out of his pocket, Johnny stepped close behind him and put his hands on Ryan's hips. Ryan paused, his key unmoving in the lock as Johnny reached around to palm Ryan's dick through his jeans. Happy to find a nice hard erection waiting for him, Johnny squeezed it through the fabric. It was a good size too, thick and substantial. Johnny's cock perked up in anticipation. He hoped Ryan would be up for fucking him, but even if he wasn't it would be a nice dick to go down on.

He kissed Ryan on the back of the neck and Ryan sucked in a breath. "You gonna let us in then?" Johnny asked, lips moving on Ryan's skin. "Or do you want to turn around and let me blow you out here?"

That galvanised Ryan into movement, turning the key, and then pushing the door open. Johnny released his grip on Ryan's dick as they stumbled inside. He kicked the door shut behind them, plunging them into total blackness without the streetlights, and reached for Ryan in the dark, snagging the back of his T-shirt before he managed to get to the light switch. "Come here and kiss me."

Ryan came willingly, his hands finding Johnny's face as their lips met in a frenzied smash. Johnny laughed breathlessly before taking control. One hand in Ryan's hair, he tilted his head the way he wanted it so he could seek out his tongue. Ryan moaned, parting his lips, and letting Johnny in. He pushed Johnny back against the wall and ground their hips together. Johnny wondered whether Ryan could feel his erection. He hoped he could, so he'd remember that he was with a guy not a girl. But then as they kissed, Ryan brought his hands down to Johnny's waist and slid them up the front of his T-shirt, stroking the smooth planes of Johnny's chest and touching his nipples with his fingertips. Yeah. Ryan definitely knew Johnny wasn't a girl, and he seemed to be totally okay with it.

Lost in the kiss, Johnny was disappointed when Ryan pulled away, until he murmured, "I want to see you. You're so fucking hot."

Johnny chuckled as Ryan reached out, fumbling for the light switch. "You think so?"

"Yeah." The light was harsh, making Johnny wince and squint.

Ryan moved back close to Johnny and their gazes locked. His eyes were blue, Johnny noticed. He'd been appreciating the whole package earlier rather than studying the details. Ryan was attractive in a very masculine, clean-cut kind of way. Tall and broad, with brown wavy hair cut short at the back and sides, he looked like he should be modelling for Jack Wills. He was very different to Johnny, and very much Johnny's type. His lips were wet from their kisses, and Johnny wanted more. He grabbed the front of Ryan's T-shirt and pulled him into another kiss, turning him so that now Ryan was the one with his back to the wall. They snogged, deep and hungry, and full of intent. Johnny reached down and rubbed Ryan's dick again. *Wow*, he was hung.

Impatient to get a closer look, he broke the kiss, and dropped to his knees. Hands on the button of Ryan's jeans, he looked up. "This okay? Is anyone in the house?"

"No. Yes. I mean.... Yeah it's okay. The others are all next door I think." Ryan's eyes were glazed with arousal and Johnny loved how desperate he looked.

Turning his attention back to Ryan's crotch, he quickly unbuttoned, unzipped, and freed his cock from his underwear. It sprung out, thick and heavy, and Johnny didn't waste any time in getting it into his mouth. He sucked on the head at first, using his hand to stroke at the same time.

Ryan groaned and there was a thud as his head hit the wall behind him. He started to move his hips, tentatively as though he was trying to stop himself from thrusting into Johnny's mouth, fists clenched by his sides.

Johnny pulled off. "It's okay. Make me take it. I like that."

"Yeah?" Ryan looked down at him.

"Yeah. Give it to me. Show me what you want."

"Fuck," Ryan said roughly. "Okay."

He put one hand around the back of Johnny's neck and used his other hand to guide his cock back into Johnny's eager mouth. Hands free now, Johnny made quick work of his own fly and moaned around his mouthful of dick as he started to stroke himself.

Ryan pushed in deep, the hand on Johnny's neck firm but not forceful. Johnny hummed and sucked enthusiastically to show Ryan he was into this. Fuck, he loved it. Ryan thrust in harder, his cock nudging the back of Johnny's throat insistently. Johnny took it for a while, but soon it was too much and he gagged, eyes watering. Ryan pulled back immediately. "Sorry."

"Nah, it's okay. I like it." Johnny took Ryan back into his mouth and drew him deep, forcing his throat to relax as Ryan started to fuck his mouth again.

They carried on like that for a little while, Ryan's moans and muttered curses a counterpoint to the wet sounds of Johnny's mouth. Eventually, Ryan said, "I'm gonna come if we keep doing this."

Johnny pulled off, stroking Ryan lightly with a hand as he asked, "Do you want to come yet?"

"I don't know." Ryan cupped Johnny's cheek and rubbed at his lower lip with his thumb. "What else is on offer?"

"My arse. If you want?"

"Yes," Ryan said immediately. "God yes. I want to fuck you so badly. Only...." His face fell. "I don't have any lube."

Johnny stood and kissed him lightly on the lips as reached into his back pocket. "Lucky for you I'm always prepared." He pressed a sachet of lube and a condom into Ryan's hand. "Upstairs?"

"Yeah."

They rearranged their clothing and Johnny followed Ryan upstairs to the first floor. Ryan pushed open a door and turned the light on. "This is my room."

It was a typical student room, fairly tidy, with a desk containing a few books, notepads, and a laptop; a wardrobe; a chest of drawers; and a large bed made up with dark blue sheets and a duvet. As Johnny looked around, Ryan put the lube and condom down on the bedside table, turned a lamp on, then came back to turn off the main light. He put his arms around Johnny and kissed him again, reaching down to squeeze Johnny's arse. He traced the crack with his fingertips, sending a thrill of arousal to Johnny's balls as he imagined those fingers opening him up for Ryan's gorgeous cock.

Reluctant to kill the mood, but preferring to be safe rather than sorry, Johnny drew away, and asked. "Can I use your bathroom for a quick clean up first? Then my arse is all yours."

"Oh, um. Sure. Need a towel?"

"Yes please."

Ryan got one from a drawer and gave it to him. "Bathroom is two doors down."

"Thanks. Why don't you get naked and warm the bed up while you wait for me," Johnny suggested with a grin. He gave Ryan's dick a quick squeeze.

"Okay." Ryan looked nervous.

"You sure you want to do this? I can just go back to sucking you off if you prefer?"

"No. I want to." Ryan's voice was firm, despite the tension rolling off him.

"Back in a minute then."

Johnny hadn't been planning on hooking up tonight otherwise he would've douched. A quick rinse with the showerhead would have to do. Once he was satisfied, he dried off, wrapped the towel around his waist, and carried his clothes back to Ryan's room. "Hey." He paused in the doorway, feeling a little awkward now the mood had been broken.

"Hey." Ryan was lying on the bed, the covers up to his waist. One hand was moving under the duvet in an obvious jerking motion as he let his gaze roam over Johnny. The hunger in his eyes made it clear he wasn't having second thoughts. "Get over here."

Johnny dumped his clothes, shut the door, and flipped the lock just in case. Then he walked over to the foot of the bed.

"Show me," he said, staring at the movement of Ryan's hand.

"If you'll show me yours." Ryan grinned.

Johnny unfastened the towel and let it drop. His cock was at half-mast after the chilly bathroom, but as Ryan stared at it, it started to crank its way back up even without Johnny touching it. "Your turn."

Ryan kicked the duvet down and revealed his glorious cock, standing to attention as Ryan stroked it slowly. "Can I see your arse?" he asked.

"Cock not doing it for you?" Johnny couldn't help being a little disappointed. Straight guys often weren't into reciprocal dick sucking, but he'd been hoping Ryan might want the full shebang.

"Nah, it is actually, more than I expected. I'm an arse man though. So...." Ryan grinned and held up the finger of his free hand, spinning it slowly.

Johnny chuckled and turned obediently. "So?" He

looked back over his shoulder as he wiggled his butt. "Does *this* do it for you?"

"Oh fuck, yes." Ryan moved over and patted the bed beside him. "Get that arse over here."

Johnny crawled onto the dark blue sheets. "How do you want me?"

"On your front."

Settling down beside him, Johnny lay flat, his face turned towards Ryan. "Like this?"

"That'll do for starters." Ryan sat up and moved down the bed. He kneed Johnny's legs apart so he could fit between them and then Johnny felt warm hands grip his arse and squeeze. "Your arse is gorgeous."

"Thanks." Johnny smiled, tilting his hips up invitingly. "Take a closer look."

Ryan parted Johnny's arse cheeks and Johnny's whole body tingled with a rush of arousal. He loved the feeling of being inspected, on display for Ryan's approval.

"You like being rimmed?" Ryan asked.

"I love it."

"Awesome." And with that, Ryan lowered himself and licked up Johnny's taint to his hole in a hot, wet slide that made Johnny's toes curl and his back arch.

"Oh fuck," he hissed, pushing up on his elbows and letting his head drop. "Yeah. Do that again." Ryan did, several times, until he finally stayed with his tongue lapping at Johnny's hole. Johnny groaned, fingers digging into the sheets as he pushed back into the sensation. Ryan's stubble rasped against his skin. "God you're good at that. I take it this isn't your first time?"

"No." Ryan paused long enough to reply, his breath hot. "I had one girlfriend who was into it."

"Only one?"

"Yeah." Ryan dived back in, circling his tongue before pressing in deeper.

"Well the others were missing out, because *damn*—" Johnny gave up on words and went back to moaning like a slut. He loved being rimmed, it was one of his favourite things and Ryan was eating his arse like he was starving for it. Time lost all meaning as Johnny lost himself in the warm, slick press of Ryan's tongue and the bite of his fingers in Johnny's arse cheeks. Eyes closed, face down on the bed, he gave himself up to Ryan, letting him set the pace now. Where before Johnny had been the one in the driving seat, now Ryan was in control and Johnny was along for the ride.

Eventually Ryan introduced a finger into the mix. He drew back to ask, "Is this okay?" as he pressed it against Johnny's eager hole.

"Yes," Johnny managed, and then gasped as Ryan pushed it inside. Aching to be fucked now, Johnny squeezed around it. "That's good. But I want more."

"Yeah?" Ryan's voice was soft and husky. "What do you want?"

"I want your cock."

"It's really thick. Most girls don't want it in their arse. You sure you can take it?"

Johnny looked over his shoulder. He was expecting to see a cocky expression, but Ryan's face was serious and Johnny realised it was a genuine question. "I can take it," he assured him. "Just go slow at first, but it won't take me long to get used to it. I've had plenty of practice."

"Okay." Ryan withdrew his finger and moved to get the lube and condom.

Johnny pushed himself up onto his knees and elbows and reached one hand down for his cock. He was hard and wet, it probably wouldn't take him long to come even after all the alcohol he'd drunk. He stroked himself slowly as Ryan put the condom on and tore open the lube. He looked back to see Ryan smearing lube on his dick, then he used his fingertips to spread what was left around Johnny's hole. The lube was cool on Johnny's hot skin and as Ryan pressed his fingers inside a little Johnny pushed back, taking more.

"Fuck, you look so hot." Ryan thrust them in and out slowly.

"You gonna fuck me then?" Johnny said. "I'm ready."

"Yeah." Ryan withdrew his fingers and slapped Johnny on the arse. "Roll over though."

Surprised, Johnny complied, turning onto his back, and drawing his knees up ready. Guys who were used to being with girls usually liked doggy style. It was less confronting, maybe. But Ryan's gaze dropped to Johnny's cock and he hesitated for a moment before taking it in his hand and tentatively stroking. He didn't grip tight enough for Johnny's liking, but it felt good anyway. Feeling vulnerable waiting with his legs spread, Johnny turned to teasing as a defence mechanism. "Any time you like."

Ryan looked at him and flushed. "Yeah, sorry. Got distracted there for a minute." He let go of Johnny's cock and lined his up instead before pushing slowly inside.

Johnny welcomed the stretch, but then tensed at the familiar ache as his muscles protested when Ryan went in a little deeper. "Wait," he bit out. "Just give me a minute."

Ryan stopped immediately. "You okay?"

"Yeah. Just hurts for now but it won't last." He took his cock in his hand. It had softened a little but firmed up again quickly as he stroked. The solid pressure of Ryan inside him started to feel better again. "Give me a little more."

Slowly and steadily, Ryan worked his way in, rocking his hips until Johnny could feel Ryan's balls pressed up snug against him with every careful thrust. Ryan was still being gentle, and the concentration on his face was endearing. "That feel okay?" His blue eyes were fixed on Johnny's face.

"Yeah." Johnny smiled. "Feels great. C'mere." He curled his hand around Ryan's nape and drew him down so their bodies were in contact while he took Ryan's mouth in a slow, thorough kiss. Ryan was still rocking into him, each deep thrust of his cock felt amazing. When Ryan eventually drew away from Johnny's mouth to kiss his neck, Johnny gripped his arse, and whispered into his ear, "Now fuck me hard. As hard as you can."

Ryan obliged, pushing himself up again he held Johnny's legs as he slammed into him. "Fuck," he gasped. "Your arse feels amazing."

"Your cock feels pretty great too," Johnny assured him, then moaned loudly as Ryan changed the angle slightly and hit Johnny exactly right. "Oh fuck!" Johnny grabbed his cock and started to stroke it hard and fast, the tension of impending orgasm building in his balls. "Yes, fuck. Like that. Don't stop."

Ryan gave a breathless chuckle. "Wasn't planning on it. Unless you want me to? I'm pretty close though."

"I don't care, I am too."

"I want to see you come first."

"Well keep fucking me hard then." Johnny's hand flew over his cock as Ryan pounded his arse. Concentrating on the sensations rather than talking now, Johnny couldn't keep quiet. Each thrust of Ryan's cock knocked a moan out of him, getting louder and more high-pitched as he felt the rising tide of climax. He teetered deliciously on the brink for a moment before it consumed him and he came with a cry, body tensing and releasing as he spilled all over his stomach and fist.

"Fuck," Ryan gasped. He carried on fucking Johnny through it, until with a final deep thrust his rhythm faltered and he came too, hips jerking and flexing. "Oh fuck, *yes*."

Ryan collapsed on top of Johnny, the weight of his body solid and grounding and his breath hot in Johnny's ear. Johnny wrapped his arms around him and inhaled the scent of his skin as his heart gradually slowed.

As Ryan's cock softened and began to slip free, he heaved himself up to guide it out and tied off the condom before tossing it into the bin by the desk. He lay back down beside Johnny, no longer touching him, and Johnny missed the warmth and contact of his body.

"That was awesome," Ryan said.

"Yeah?" Johnny rolled to his side and propped himself on one elbow to study Ryan.

He didn't meet Johnny's gaze, eyes fixed on the ceiling. But he nodded. "Yeah. It was so hot." He looked at Johnny then and grinned. "You have a hot arse."

"Thanks." Johnny smirked. "You certainly made good use of it."

Heat flared in Ryan's eyes. "Yeah. I guess I did." He went back to staring at the ceiling, so Johnny turned onto his back again. His body felt like a collection of limp noodles. Fucked out and exhausted now the alcohol was starting to wear off, he yawned hugely. "I should go and clean up a bit. I'm covered in jizz." He got up and picked up the towel he'd used before. "Back in a minute."

When he returned, less sticky than before, Ryan was in bed with his eyes closed. He had a T-shirt on now and looked so comfortable that Johnny frowned. It wasn't fair that he got to fall asleep when Johnny had to walk home in the dark and the cold. He pulled on his underwear and his T-shirt, and was about to put on his jeans too, when Ryan said in a sleepy voice, "You can stay here if you want."

"Really?"

"Yeah. If you feel anything like I do right now you probably don't fancy walking home."

"It's not the most appealing thought, you're right."

"So stay. I don't mind, and I promise not to molest you in your sleep."

Johnny's arse muscles clenched reflexively at the thought. "I wouldn't mind if you did."

Ryan chuckled. "I'm too tired for round two."

"Shame," Johnny said lightly.

Decision made, he slipped under the covers beside Ryan. Johnny didn't often sleep over with hook ups, but occasionally he did if he felt safe with them and was feeling lazy. He definitely felt safe with Ryan, partly because there was a friend-of-a-friend connection, but mainly because Ryan gave off a definite nice-guy vibe. Johnny trusted him, so he'd be able to relax enough to get a decent night's sleep. As he snuggled under the duvet, Ryan reached over to turn off the lamp by the bed before rolling back to lie beside Johnny.

"Night then," Ryan said quietly.

"Night."

THREE

Ryan woke with a mouth that felt like it was lined with dirty carpet, a thumping headache, a full bladder, and an annoyingly insistent erection. "Ugh." He flopped onto his back and his elbow bumped a warm body beside him.

What the fuck?

Cranking his eyes open, Ryan looked at the person in his bed. Silky blond hair spread across the pillowcase, and for a split second Ryan thought he was in bed with a girl. But then the events of the previous night ground into place like rusty gears and Ryan's heart thumped hard when he realised it was Johnny beside him. Beautiful, fascinating, Johnny with his devastating smile and ridiculously hot arse.

The need to piss finally drove Ryan to move. He got up as quietly as he could without jostling the bed, not wanting to deal with an awkward morning-after conversation until he'd had a chance to piss and brush his teeth because he'd clearly passed out without doing that last night. He must have been fairly drunk; the fruity stuff Johnny had been drinking had been strong.

In the bathroom, Ryan willed his dick to deflate enough

so he could empty his bladder. That pressing need met, he looked at himself in the mirror. *Jesus*, he looked rough as fuck. His blue eyes were bloodshot and had dark circles underneath them. Rubbing his hands over his stubbled cheeks, he wrinkled his nose when he remembered he'd crashed out without washing after rimming and fingering Johnny the night before.

Eww.

But as Ryan turned on the tap and waited for the water to run hot, he was assaulted by a vivid visual memory of Johnny's perfect little arse cheeks, spread wide by Ryan's hands, and that pink hole just inviting Ryan to lick it. The thought of his tongue in Johnny's arse made heat trickle through Ryan and his cock started to perk up again. God it had been amazing. Definitely one of the best hook ups Ryan had ever had. Good to know sex with a guy could be fun, even if it wasn't something Ryan necessarily wanted to do again. He felt weird knowing that Johnny was still in his bed though. Ryan didn't know what he'd been thinking last night when he'd told Johnny he could stay. Ryan never let hook ups sleep over. He'd walk a girl home rather than let her sleep in his bed, unless they were dating. He liked his space and his privacy and waking up next to some random you weren't planning on seeing again was always awkward. When that person was a guy it was probably going to be a whole new level of awkward.

He washed his hands and face, and brushed his teeth before returning to his room. Johnny was still almost out of sight under the duvet apart from the tangle of blond hair on the pillow. Ryan deliberately pulled the door shut with a thud, hoping it would wake Johnny up.

Sure enough, Johnny groaned. Pushing the covers down

a little, he lifted his head, and blinked sleepily at Ryan. "Oh, hey, Ryan," he croaked.

At least he could remember Ryan's name despite the alcohol. He was still unfairly hot considering he'd just woken up. Sure, he looked like he'd been dragged through a hedge backwards but it was a good look on him. With his messy hair falling in eyes that were rimmed with smudges of black eyeliner, he looked like a decadent rock star after a heavy night. As he sat up, the covers fell away and pale skin showed where the neck of his T-shirt dipped low.

A frisson of arousal made Ryan turn away and grab a pair of jeans to pull on. He'd been hoping Johnny's charms would be diluted in the cold light of the morning, or that he would have fucked last night's bi-curiosity out of his system.

Apparently neither of those things had happened.

"You got somewhere you need to be?" Johnny's voice was casual.

"Um. Not particularly. I just don't like lying around in bed once I'm awake. And I'm hungry." That part was true at least. Ryan's stomach growled at the thought of food. He usually liked to feed a hangover; it would settle his uneasy belly.

"I should probably get out of your hair then." Ryan didn't reply, keeping his back to Johnny as he heard the creak of the bed and the rustle of the duvet, then Johnny's voice again asking, "What time is it?"

Ryan looked at his watch. "Nearly eleven."

"Fuck. That late? You must have worn me out for me to have slept so long."

Ryan turned just in time to see Johnny's tight little arse in snug red boxers, the bright colour a surprising contrast to the rest of his clothes. *Damn that's hot*. He hadn't noticed Johnny's underwear last night, but then Johnny had done most of the work, he recalled with a flash of guilt. Ryan had been a pretty selfish fuck. But Johnny had seemed to enjoy himself regardless.

Johnny pulled up his skinny black jeans, and Ryan looked away quickly, picking up a hoodie from the back of his desk chair to put on. Johnny carried on dressing in silence, sitting on the bed to pull on his boots and do up the laces.

Once they were both fully dressed, Ryan felt less vulnerable around Johnny. Not wanting to be a total arsehole, he said tentatively, "Do you want a cup of tea or coffee, or anything to eat?"

Johnny studied him for an uncomfortable moment before saying, "Nah, man. I'm just gonna head off."

Ryan felt a rush of mingled regret and relief, as though he was letting something slip away that maybe he should try and hang on to.

It's just a hook up, he told himself firmly. *Don't be ridiculous.*

"Okay. Well... thanks. I guess," he said awkwardly. "Last night was fun."

"Yeah." Johnny was still looking at him, and his cool grey gaze made Ryan feel hot and flustered. "You're a good fuck. How do you feel about your little foray over the rainbow?" His lips curved in a teasing smile, but Ryan sensed a tension in the air as Johnny waited for his reply.

It was too soon for Ryan to answer that honestly even if he wanted to. He hadn't had time to process it yet, so he went with being flippant. "Yeah, it was hot. Turns out it doesn't make too much difference to me what junk comes with a nice arse as part of the package. And it's always fun to try something new."

Johnny snorted. "Another tick on your sexual bucket list?"

"Something like that." Ryan tried to grin but it felt forced.

"I like to think of it as a public service I provide—although if I had a pound for every *straight* guy I've fucked I'd have enough to eat for a week I reckon."

Ryan gave an awkward laugh. "Yeah, well. More of us are sexually flexible than we like to admit."

"No shit." Looking around the room, Johnny frowned. "Oh bollocks. I left my jacket next door last night. Okay. I'm gonna leave you to your sexual identity crisis. Thanks for the fuck." He rounded the bed and stopped in front of Ryan. With Johnny in his boots and Ryan in bare feet, they were exactly the same height. Johnny put a hand on Ryan's shoulder, leaned in quickly, and brushed the barest of kisses on Ryan's cheek. "See you around, maybe. Bye for now."

"Yeah. Bye."

Ryan stared dumbly at the door as it closed behind Johnny. His cheek tingled where Johnny's lips had been.

AS RYAN MADE his way downstairs, he wondered if his housemates had noticed that he'd disappeared with Johnny last night. The only people he knew for sure had seen them together were Ben and Sid. Ryan hadn't exactly been subtle about his interest when they were dancing, though, and gossip had a habit of spreading fast among groups of friends.

It wasn't that Ryan was ashamed of hooking up with Johnny. He preferred to keep his private life relatively private even when he was hooking up with girls. But if people knew he'd hooked up with a guy they'd make all sorts of assumptions about him that Ryan wasn't comfortable with.

A burst of laughter from the kitchen made his skin crawl with paranoia. Were they talking about him?

Squaring his shoulders, Ryan walked into the kitchen and forced himself to look casual. Three of his five housemates were in there, Nadia was making toast, and Colin and James were vying for space at the hob. The smell of frying bacon and eggs was thick in the air and Ryan's stomach clenched with hunger.

"Morning all," he said breezily.

He was greeted by various hi's and good mornings.

"Hey, Ryan," Nadia said. "You didn't stay at the party very late."

"Yeah, I was tired," Ryan said noncommittally. "Damn, that bacon smells good. Where's mine?" He went up to lean over James's shoulder to see four rashers sizzling in a sea of oil alongside an egg, while Colin was stirring baked beans in one pan and scrambling eggs in another.

"Fuck off and make your own." James nudged him in the ribs to get him to back off.

"Harsh." Ryan flicked his ear. "I'm sure you owe me from last weekend. Didn't I make you cheese and onion toasties after the pub when you didn't have any decent food in?"

"Hmm.... Yeah, okay. You can have two bits of bacon then, but this is all I've got, and I'm out of eggs. Make yourself useful and spread some marg on bread for sandwiches then. I forgot to do that first."

Ryan busied himself with that, grateful for something to do.

"Hi, everyone," Justine said, coming into the kitchen.

She went straight to the kettle and switched it on. "Anyone need tea or coffee?"

"Tea please," Ryan said, looking up from the bread.

Justine turned away, getting a couple of mugs out of a cupboard. "Nadia, did you pull that blond guy from the party last night?"

Ryan froze, knife stilling as he gripped it tight in his hand.

"What blond guy?" Nadia asked.

"That one you said was hot, the tall one with long hair."

"Oh, God. No. I wish. I asked Ewan about him but apparently he's gay so I didn't even try. I think he left early anyway."

"Did he crash here though? Because I met him on the landing when I came out of the bathroom."

"When?" Nadia frowned.

"About five minutes ago."

Deciding it was better to face this head-on, Ryan cleared his throat. Face flaming, he admitted, "Um. He slept in my room."

Nadia's eyes flew wide. "Oh my God, did *you* hook up with him?"

A few seconds ticked by, filled only with the sound of the kettle, the fan over the cooker, and the sizzle of bacon, as Ryan's flatmates waited for his reply.

Ryan shrugged, trying to look casual but feeling about a million miles away from achieving it. "Yeah."

Another pause.

James was the one to finally break the silence with a nervous chuckle. "You're having a laugh."

"No. I hooked up with him. Why, have you got a problem with that?" Ryan turned and met James's gaze, raising his eyebrows.

"Not at all. I'm just... surprised that's all. I didn't think you swung that way."

"I don't. Well... I mean, I don't usually. But one thing led to another, and I thought—why not?"

"A hole's a hole I guess," James said, then he snorted. "Assuming you weren't the one on the receiving end."

"No!" Ryan snapped, an unwelcome vision of him bending over for Johnny flashing into his consciousness. "No, I'm definitely not into that."

"Good." James went back to poking the bacon and flipped his egg over.

"Have you ever tried it?" Nadia asked. "And if not, then how would you know? My ex thought he wouldn't like things up his arse, but I dared him to try and he ended up loving it."

"Look, can we stop this conversation now please?" Ryan turned back to buttering the bread. "My arse is my business, and it's strictly exit only, thank you very much. And my private life is my business too, so butt out."

Colin snorted. "No pun intended."

"So it was just a one-off then?" Nadia asked. "You and the hot blond—what's his name anyway?"

"Johnny. And yes," he said decisively. They hadn't exchanged numbers or even hinted at a repeat performance, and that was probably for the best. Ryan didn't have time for complications in his life with his finals approaching.

"And is he definitely gay, not bi?" A shred of hope crept into Nadia's voice.

"I don't know. I didn't ask him."

"Hmm... maybe I should see if I can get more information from the guys next door."

"Yeah, Ben would know." Irked at Nadia's interest in

Johnny, Ryan was desperate to get off the topic now. "That bacon nearly done, James?"

"Yes. It's ready." James turned off the pan and they assembled their sandwiches.

The conversation between the others turned to someone who had fallen over drunk and twisted their ankle at the party last night, and Ryan was glad he was no longer the focus of the gossip.

THAT EVENING, Ryan had given up on studying and was searching for male models on Pinterest—for science. He wanted to see whether he fancied men in general, or Johnny specifically. A little bit of research confirmed that hooking up with Johnny last night had unlocked something for sure. After years of not thinking about guys in a sexual way, Ryan found that he did find some men attractive, but only a very specific type. The more androgynous-looking the better and he definitely had a thing for blonds.

He was trying to decide how he felt about this development when there was a knock on his bedroom door.

Quickly switching tabs on his browser, before spinning around on his desk chair, Ryan said, "Yeah?"

It was Ewan. "Hi. Can I come in?"

Ryan didn't know why Ewan bothered asking, because he was already closing the door behind him. "Sure. What's up?" He was fairly sure he knew what was up, but he wanted Ewan to ask rather than him volunteer the information. Ewan flopped down on Ryan's bed, propping himself up on the pillows. "Make yourself at home."

"Thanks." Ewan grinned. "So. You and Johnny. What's going on there?"

Ryan sighed. "Who told you?"

"Straight from the horse's mouth, mate."

"What? Johnny told you? Fuck's sake." Ryan knew he'd gone next door that morning to get his jacket. But he didn't think Johnny would have dropped him in it. He knew it was Ryan's first time with a guy, and although Ryan hadn't asked him to be discreet… well. He didn't think he'd have to spell it out.

"No. To be fair, he didn't actually tell us. His exact words were that he doesn't kiss and tell. But Sid had seen him with you, and Johnny didn't deny it after that."

"Oh." Mollified, Ryan relaxed a little. The cat was already out of the bag after the conversation in the kitchen earlier, so it didn't really make much difference if Ewan and the guys next door knew too.

"So… back to my original question. What's going on with you and Johnny?" Ewan crossed his arms over his chest and waited expectantly.

"Nothing. I mean… yeah, we hooked up, but that's all. I doubt I'll be seeing him again—not like that anyway."

"Just a one-off then?"

"I assume so."

"But that was a first for you, no? With another guy I mean?"

"Yes."

"Are you freaking out?" Ewan narrowed his eyes.

Ryan shrugged, thinking about the models he'd been looking at on Pinterest. Did that count as freaking out? He still wasn't sure what difference it made. Just because he thought girly-looking guys were sometimes hot didn't mean much. It wasn't exactly a game-changer as far as his life plan was concerned. Ryan had always assumed he'd eventually find a woman he liked enough to settle down with, and would get married and have two-point-four kids, and maybe a dog. Dogs were cool. Having a vague interest in femme men didn't mean a rethink. If he wanted, he could fuck that out of his system before he settled down, and after that, there was always porn.

"Ryan?"

Ewan's voice snapped Ryan back to the present away from his imaginary future. He realised he'd picked at a bit of skin by his thumbnail so much it was bleeding, and he still hadn't answered Ewan's question.

"Yeah. I guess I'm freaking out a little bit," Ryan admitted. He put his thumb in his mouth to suck the blood off, avoiding Ewan's gaze.

"Did you enjoy it? Whatever you did with Johnny?"

"I fucked him," Ryan said bluntly, not wanting Ewan to think it had been the other way around. "And yeah. It was...." He considered for a moment. *Amazing, disturbing, worryingly hot.* "Good," he finished lamely. "I just don't know what to think about it now. I mean, I like girls. I've always liked girls. So I didn't expect to enjoy it as much as I did."

"Look," Ewan said firmly. "One experience of gay sex doesn't make you gay. It's not what you do with your dick that determines your sexuality; it's what you *want* to do with it that matters. So if you want to fuck guys as well as girls now, well maybe you're bi. And if you are? Well, it's not a huge deal is it? Not in this day and age. So don't stress about it. If it's something you want to explore further then you can, and if not—move on and chalk it up to experience."

"Yeah. You're right." Ryan gave Ewan a small smile. "Cheers, mate." Then he chuckled. "Look at you talking sense for once."

"Wow. Hurtful." Ewan clutched his chest in mock distress.

"Nah, seriously. Thanks for the pep talk."

Ewan got up and punched Ryan lightly on the shoulder. "You're welcome, man. It's what gay BFFs are for. I'll leave you to your work now. I hope it helped."

"Yeah, it did."

Ewan closed the door as he left, and Ryan leaned back in his desk chair and re-opened the tab with the blond male models. None of them were as hot as Johnny anyway.

Move on and chalk it up to experience.

That sounded like a plan. How hard could it be?

FOUR

April (two months later)

"CHEERS, GUYS," Johnny said as Jez and Jude dumped the boxes they were carrying down on the floor of his new room.

"No worries. Is this everything?" Jez asked.

"Nah. There's a few more things coming in a final load later. But this is most of it now." Johnny looked around at the boxes, assorted bags, and bin liners full of his crap. He wasn't sure how he'd managed to accumulate so much stuff in the time he'd been sharing a flat with Sid. It was amazing how it mounted up.

"I'm afraid I'm going out later, so I won't be around to help," Jez said.

"Yeah, me too." Jude gave a rueful grin. "I promised Shawn I'd meet him at the gym after he finishes work."

"No worries, honestly. I can manage. I appreciate you helping with the first car load."

"Well have fun unpacking," Jez said. "See you later."

"Welcome to the madhouse." Jude offered Johnny a fist to bump.

Johnny laughed. "Thanks, man."

Left alone, he looked around his new place.

It had been his suggestion to swap with Ben. Since Sid and Ben had got together, Ben had spent so much time over at their flat it was like having three of them living there. Johnny didn't mind. He liked Ben, but it did get a little tiring playing third wheel to a happy couple. Not that he'd totally escaped couples by moving into the large shared house that was his new home; Jez and Mac were together, and so were Shawn and Jude. And Johnny's fifth housemate, Dev, was in a relationship with Ewan who lived in the house next door to this one. But at least with more of them around, the PDAs might be more diluted, and Johnny wouldn't feel so much like a spare part.

At the thought of the neighbouring house, Johnny felt a prickle of unease. His only worry about moving here was that now he'd be living next door to Ryan.

Memories of their night together still lingered, nagging at the edges of Johnny's consciousness. Ryan had been a really great fuck, but the morning after was uncomfortable. Usually Johnny was able to shrug these things off and move on, but something about Ryan had got under his skin. He was far from the first bi-curious guy that Johnny had hooked up with. He enjoyed messing with their heads and watching their preconceived notions about themselves come crashing down. Normally, he'd forget about them and happily move on to the next conquest. But Ryan had left Johnny wanting more and Johnny hated wanting things he couldn't have.

He'd deliberately made no effort to contact Ryan, knowing that Ryan could easily track him down if he wanted. Of course he hadn't—why would he? Johnny was just an experiment for him, an enjoyable one maybe, but that was all.

A couple of weeks after they'd hooked up, he'd seen Ryan in town one day. They'd been walking in opposite directions through the shopping centre and passed within a few feet of each other. Their gazes had met, and Johnny had given Ryan a smile and nod in greeting. But Ryan hadn't responded in kind. Shocked recognition had flashed in his eyes before he looked away quickly, head down as he hurried away. It had been a sharp kick in Johnny's guts to be ignored like that, like he was nothing—or worse, like he was something that Ryan regretted.

Arsehole.

Living next door to Ryan, there was no way they were going to be able to avoid each other. Johnny hoped they could get past the awkwardness quickly and forget about what had happened between them. He tried to push aside the hurt and anger he still felt when he remembered Ryan blanking him in the street, but his sense of unease remained as he began to unpack.

Johnny had only managed to sort out a couple of boxes when his phone buzzed with a text from Dana, Sid's friend from work, who was helping them move:

I'm parked outside again, wanna come down?

Johnny left the box of books he was in the middle of emptying and went down to find her double-parked with her hazard lights on.

"Hey. I would offer to help you carry stuff up, but I daren't leave the car unattended because I'm blocking the road."

"No worries," Johnny said. "Just give me a hand to unload onto the pavement then you can head off."

"You sure? I don't mind waiting if you want to get it inside."

"No, it's fine."

It was a smaller load this time, just a suitcase, a few more boxes, and several carrier bags stuffed full of clothes that wouldn't fit in Johnny's case. They lined them up along the wall that separated the small front yards of the houses from the street.

"That's the last ones." Dana put down the carrier bags she was holding.

With perfect timing, a taxi drove down the street and beeped its horn insistently when it had to stop behind Dana's car.

"Thanks so much for helping," Johnny said as she hurried away.

"You're welcome," she called over her shoulder. "Good luck with the unpacking."

As Johnny stooped to lift the first box, he heard voices and footsteps approaching rapidly from down the street. Recognising Ryan's voice, he stiffened. Straightening up, he turned to meet the source of the sound. Ryan and a stocky, sandy-haired guy Johnny recognised, but whose name he couldn't remember, were jogging towards him.

They stopped by the path to their front door, just a few feet away from him.

"Hi," the sandy-haired guy said. "Johnny, isn't it? Are you moving in?"

"Hi. And yeah." Johnny gripped the box tightly, tension coiling in his muscles as he let his gaze slide to Ryan. "Ben's moving into my flat with Sid, so we're doing a swap."

Flushed, sweaty, and wearing sports clothes and trainers, Ryan looked annoyingly hot. He also looked less than thrilled at the prospect of having Johnny as a neighbour.

Breaking the awkward silence, the sandy-haired guy asked, "Do you want a hand with that lot?"

"There's no need. I can manage," Johnny said. Then realised he probably sounded rude. "But thanks."

"Don't be daft. It won't take long with three of us." Without waiting for Johnny or Ryan to agree to the arrangement, the guy came over and lifted another box while Ryan hung back uncertainly for a moment.

"Thanks, uh... I'm sorry. I don't remember your name." Johnny shifted the weight of the box in his arms, which were aching now.

"It's James. I don't think we were ever actually introduced."

Ryan finally moved, going and picking up several carrier bags as James led the way to Johnny's new front door, which was slightly ajar. Johnny followed close behind, with Ryan on his heels.

"Where do you want this?" James was already on his way upstairs.

"First door on the right," Johnny said. He was painfully aware of Ryan behind him. He must be eye level with Johnny's arse. Johnny wondered whether Ryan was thinking about the time when he'd had his tongue in it, because Johnny sure as hell was. His skin prickled at the memory and some blood redistributed itself to his dick.

James marched in and put his box down, standing aside to let the other two in before heading straight back out.

Johnny dumped his box on the bed.

"Where do you want these?" Ryan asked.

"Wherever there's a space." Johnny gestured around the chaos.

Ryan put the bags on the floor next to some other boxes, as he put them down one of them fell over and fabric spilled out of it. "Oh, shit, sorry." Ryan crouched down to shove the contents back into the bag, then froze, looking at what was in his hand.

Fuck. Johnny flushed hot when he realised Ryan was holding a pair of bright pink lace boy shorts. Boy shorts was a weird name when you thought about it, because they definitely weren't meant for boys. Johnny liked wearing them sometimes, when he was feeling in a particularly feminine mood. The lace on his skin looked and felt sexy. They were stretchy enough that he could fit his dick and balls into them, even if they weren't very comfortable to wear for long periods.

"No worries," Johnny managed, throat tight. But along with the embarrassment of Ryan seeing his lacy undies, he also felt a swoop of arousal. He wondered what Ryan would think if he saw Johnny wearing them. Would he be into it?

"Are these yours?" Ryan's voice sounded as strangled as Johnny's felt. He was still squatting on the floor, skimpy pink lace in his fist. He glanced up at Johnny questioningly.

"Yeah."

Their gazes locked for a long moment. Ryan's cheeks were flushed and there was a hunger in his eyes that went straight to Johnny's cock. Johnny swallowed, his mouth dry.

The sound of feet on the stairs galvanised Ryan into action. He shoved the underwear deep into the bag they'd fallen out of and straightened up, adjusting his dick as he did so. Johnny caught the movement and gave him a knowing grin just as James barrelled through the door carrying two boxes stacked on top of each other.

"What kept you? Slackers."

"Sorry," Johnny said smoothly, his confidence back in place like a shield. "We had a mishap with a bag. Didn't mean to leave you to do all the work."

"Yeah. I'm on it." Ryan hurried out, and Johnny followed him down. James wasn't far behind, so Johnny couldn't have said anything else to Ryan even if he'd wanted to.

There wasn't much stuff left outside.

"You can manage that without me as I've already done an extra load," James said. "I'm heading in to shower. I reek." He sniffed his armpits. "Five-a-side always makes me sweat like a bitch. See you later, Ryan. Good to meet you again, Johnny."

"You too. Thanks for the help."

"You're welcome."

Left alone, Johnny and Ryan carried the last load up in silence.

Ryan put the bags he was carrying down, carefully this time as though worried about what other secrets he might inadvertently reveal, and then ran a hand through his hair. "So, um. Good luck with the unpacking. And welcome to the street I guess."

"Are you going to ignore me when we run into each other? Or will you actually say hi to me now we're neighbours?" Johnny raised his eyebrows in challenge, unable to stop a hint of bitterness creeping into his tone.

Ryan flushed and winced. "Yeah. I'm sorry about that. I just…. You kind of blindsided me that day. I didn't mean to be an arsehole."

"Do you always ignore people you've hooked up with? Or only the guys?"

"You're the only guy I've hooked up with. I told you that."

Johnny shrugged. "You might have hooked up with more since."

"I haven't."

"Decided it's not for you?"

Ryan gave an exasperated sigh. "Do you always ask people such difficult questions?"

"Yes." Johnny stuck his hands in his pockets. "Life's too short for bullshit. And if we're going to be living next door to each other I'd rather not feel awkward every time I see you in the street. So, are we good?"

"Yeah. We're good."

They stared at each other. Johnny thought Ryan would be in a hurry to get away, but he seemed to be lingering and Johnny wished he knew what was going through his head. On impulse he asked, "Do you want to go out for a drink sometime? Show me which pubs are decent around here?"

Ryan's eyes widened. "Uh. I guess we could. When were you thinking?"

"Well. I need to unpack tonight. But what about tomorrow? I know it's a Sunday but we don't need to be out late. Just a quiet drink to clear the air while you show me the local sights."

"Okay," Ryan said. "What time?"

"Seven?"

"All right. I would offer to swap numbers but I haven't got my phone on me."

"I'll give you mine. Hang on...." Johnny located a Sharpie he'd used to label some of his boxes. "Oh. Fuck knows where there's some paper though."

"Write it on my hand." Ryan offered.

"It won't wash off easily."

"Well then I won't lose it before I put it on my phone. Here."

Ryan moved close enough that Johnny could smell him, fresh masculine sweat cutting through deodorant. He held out his hand, palm down. Johnny gripped it as he wrote his number on the back. Ryan's hand was warm, big, and broad compared to Johnny's. Johnny suppressed a shiver of excitement as he remembered how it had felt to be touched by him.

"There you go." He released Ryan's hand and smiled.

"See you tomorrow then." Ryan grinned back.

As the door closed behind him, Johnny sat on the edge of the bed and tried to work out what had just happened.

Did I just ask him on a date?

He wasn't sure, honestly. But whatever he'd offered, Ryan had said yes.

FIVE

What the fuck was that?

Ryan ran over the conversation he'd just had with Johnny as he let himself into his house. He went straight up to his room where he'd left his phone on charge and copied Johnny's number into his contacts. Deciding not to text immediately, he put his phone back down. He didn't want to seem too keen and give Johnny the wrong idea—or maybe the right idea? Ryan needed to sort out his thoughts before he could even tell.

Hearing the bang of the bathroom door as James vacated it, Ryan picked up his towel and went to shower.

As the hot water washed away the sweat, his mind didn't get any clearer. He scrubbed at the number on his hand with soap, and it faded, but didn't go away completely. The numbers lingered on his skin, just like his thoughts of Johnny had persisted since their hook up.

Ryan had tried hard to file away his memory of that night. To treat it as something that was over and done with, a sexy memory of a time where he'd taken a chance. He'd experimented and it had paid off, but it wasn't something he necessarily wanted to repeat. He hadn't expected to see Johnny again. Plymouth was a big city, and Ryan didn't socialise much with Ben, who was the only common link. When he'd run into Johnny in the street he'd been taken completely by surprise. So he'd been a total dick and had tried to pretend that he hadn't noticed or recognised him, but Johnny clearly hadn't been fooled for a minute.

With Johnny living next door, avoiding him wasn't going to be an option, and clearing the air seemed like a sensible idea. It wouldn't be fun for either of them if things were uncomfortable. Ryan suspected that going out for a drink with Johnny might make things more complicated rather than smoothing things over, though. Perhaps he should have declined, using revision as an excuse because his finals started in a couple of weeks. And fuck, the last thing he needed with exams coming up was more complications in his life.

Oh well. Too late now.

LATER THAT EVENING, James knocked on Ryan's door.

"How are you doing? Revision going well?"

Ryan yawned and stretched. "Yeah. I've been pretty productive tonight." A glance at the clock told him it was nearly ten. He'd managed a solid three hours since dinner and was happy with his progress. He was studying for an organic chemistry unit and had spent the evening going through the key points on index cards. It felt like the facts were sticking.

"You going to work late tonight? Or are you done? I've had it now, so I was going to have a couple of beers and watch some TV."

"Oh, that sounds good. I think my brain is done, so I'll join you."

Downstairs, they stretched out on opposite ends of the sofa. None of their other housemates were around, so they had free rein with the TV remote. They settled on some reality show, which was nicely undemanding, after deciding they didn't have the brain power left to focus on a film.

Beer in hand, Ryan put his feet up on the coffee table and sighed. Revision was a bitch. He couldn't wait till his exams were done. He had a research job lined up at the university—subject to him getting a good 2:1—starting in August, which would be a new kind of stress. But he was ready for it, looking forward to earning money and narrowing his focus into a field that really interested him.

"What's that on your hand?" James asked idly.

Ryan's heart thumped. Lost in chemistry of the non-sexual kind, he'd managed to shift his brain into a non-Johnny gear for a few hours. But James's question brought him screeching back into the realisation that this time tomorrow he'd be out with Johnny. Out *drinking* with Johnny, and the last time he and Johnny had been together with alcohol involved, things had ended interestingly.

"What does it look like?" Ryan quipped back, faux-casual.

"You pulled someone? But when? You've been in all evening."

Ryan took a swig of his beer. "Nah, not like that. It's Johnny's number actually."

"Johnny next door?"

"Yeah."

"Johnny who you hooked up with a couple of months ago and haven't seen since till today?"

"What's your point?" Ryan kept his gaze fixed on the TV.

"So are you seeing him again then? Like *seeing* him, seeing him?"

"We're just going out for a casual drink tomorrow. Things were a bit awkward today. But now he's living next door we want to clear the air. Just be mates."

James snorted. "Mates. Right."

"What?" Ryan glanced sideways, irritated. "It's only a drink. I said I'd show him the local pubs that are decent to drink in."

"Oh, okay. So if it's just a casual friendly thing then I could tag along?" James's face was the picture of innocence. "Because I wouldn't mind going out for a couple of beers tomorrow."

Ryan glared at him unsure how to respond. Because James was right, damn him. If it was only a friendly drink then it shouldn't be a problem to ask James along too, or any of their other housemates—or Johnny's. But now he'd been put on the spot, Ryan realised he'd rather have Johnny all to himself. He wanted the chance for them to get to know each other a little better, and see what it led to.

James grinned, triumphant. "I take it that's a no to me joining you then? So like I said: mates. Right. Because it's *so* easy to be mates with a guy after fucking him—not that I'd know about that—but it doesn't usually work out too well with girls. You're totally into him."

Ryan knew James well enough to be sure that he wasn't being a dick about this because Johnny was a guy. That wasn't the issue. James just liked taking the piss out of Ryan, and any excuse would do. "Fuck you. You're only jealous because you haven't been laid in even longer than me, and Heidi isn't interested." It was a low blow. Heidi was a girl on James's course who James had had a crush on forever. But she'd made it clear it was never going to happen so James was pining from afar.

"Yeah whatever. You're into him." James turned back to the TV and took a swig of his beer. He pressed a button on the remote. "Oh cool. It's time for *Match of the Day*." After switching channels, he settled back to focus on the telly instead of Ryan, thankfully.

Ryan's attention wandered as he watched the football highlights.

Am I into him?

He couldn't deny he wanted to have sex with Johnny again. Johnny was hot, and Ryan fancied him. But it would be a terrible idea to go there again, especially now Johnny lived next door. A one-off was one thing, but a repeat felt dangerous. Then again, perhaps it wouldn't be as good the second time and then it would be easier to forget about him. Sometimes it was like that. You had an amazing one-night stand, and then when you went back for more it didn't live up to expectations. Maybe he should try and hook up with Johnny again. It might get him out of his system.

"Fucking yes. That was an amazing goal!" James exclaimed loudly, and Ryan realised with a flush of embarrassment that he was ignoring the footy while angsting over the boy next door. What the hell was wrong with him? Giving himself a mental slap, he pushed Johnny out of his mind for now, deciding to go with the flow tomorrow and see what happened. Johnny might not be interested in more than a friendly drink anyway, and Ryan was stressing for nothing.

RYAN GREW PROGRESSIVELY MORE jittery as the

hours passed on Sunday. He managed to forget about Johnny and get some revision done in the morning, but by lunchtime he kept glancing at his phone. Johnny couldn't text him, so it was up to Ryan to make contact and check if Johnny still wanted to go out. Ryan half-hoped he might change his mind, but at the same time he knew he'd be gutted if he did.

He finally gave in and sent Johnny a quick text after lunch:

You still up for that drink tonight? (This is Ryan BTW)

He put his phone back in his pocket and went up to his room to try to do more revision. He'd deliberately left it on silent so he wouldn't be distracted, but he kept pulling it out to check the frustratingly blank screen, which fucked up his concentration anyway. So, he turned the sound on and left it on his desk next to the notes he was trying to memorise.

It was an hour before Johnny replied, and Ryan's heart surged with nerves and excitement as he read the brief message: *Yeah, sure. What time?*

He sent back: *7ish still okay?*

Yeah sure. Shall I call for you?

Ryan debated briefly. James already knew, but he might not blab about it to the rest of the house. He liked teasing Ryan, but he wasn't a gossip. Ewan on the other hand, and Nadia.... But then Ewan spent half his time next door anyway. Resigning himself to the fact that if anything else happened with Johnny, keeping it a total secret would be impossible, Ryan replied: *Okay. See you then*.

RYAN WAS TOO nervous to eat much before he went out. There were butterflies taking up all the available space in his stomach. He tried calming them down with a couple of pieces of toast, but it didn't help much. He felt ridiculous for getting into such a state. He hadn't been this nervous about a date since he was fourteen and meeting Suzanne Hadley in the park. And he didn't even know if this *was* a date.

Dressed in deliberately casual jeans, T-shirt, and a hoodie, he waited in the living room for the sound of the doorbell. Nadia and Justine were watching TV, and Colin was sitting at the table eating his dinner. Seven o'clock came and went, but his phone remained silent as Ryan's nerves and anticipation ramped up higher and higher. Finally, at ten past seven—although it felt like hours had passed—the doorbell rang. Ryan shot up to get it before anyone else could.

"You expecting someone?" Colin raised his eyebrows.

"Yeah. I'm off out. See you later." Ryan hurried out before Colin could ask anything else.

He took a deep breath to steady himself and opened the door.

"Hi." Johnny was standing there, blond hair gleaming in the evening sun. One hand in the pocket of his usual black skinny jeans, he looked effortlessly casual, and projected calm confidence. "How are you?" He tucked a strand of hair behind his ear and smiled. Ryan's heart skipped a beat. Johnny was so fucking pretty. With the smooth clean-shaven planes of his face, and black eyeliner ringing his grey eyes, hearing a masculine voice come out of his mouth was incongruous.

Forcing himself to be cool, Ryan stepped out to join him. "Good thanks," he said, pulling the door shut behind him. "So, where are we going then?"

"Isn't that your call?" Johnny quirked an eyebrow. "You're the one who knows the local pubs, remember?"

"Oh. Uh, yeah. Sorry." Ryan winced, cheeks burning. "I'm a bit brain-dead after revising all day."

Johnny chuckled. "No worries. So. Where to?"

"Let's try the Old Duke." Ryan started walking, and Johnny fell into step beside him. "Do you know it? It's only about five minutes' walk from here."

"I've been past it but never been in."

"It's nice in there, pretty chilled."

"Is it LGBT friendly?"

"I don't know. I think so. Ewan and Dev go there with us sometimes. We've never had any trouble, but they're pretty discreet when they're in public anyway." Ryan felt shit for not paying more attention. He knew that some people could be homophobic twats, but as it had never affected him directly he didn't tend to worry too much about where he drank.

"Even if I don't grope your dick, people will probably assume I'm gay because of how I look," Johnny said. "But if it's a place where it's mainly students and professionals rather than the more hard-arse locals we should be fine."

Ryan ignored the flash of heat he felt at the thought of Johnny groping him. "Yeah, it's definitely that sort of pub. But if you don't feel like it's a good fit when we get there just say and we can leave."

"Okay, thanks."

THE OLD DUKE turned out to be a good choice. It was fairly quiet on a Sunday evening and had a cosy feel to it. The other customers were a mixture of couples and groups, mostly in their twenties or thirties. Nobody looked twice at them when they entered and Johnny didn't stand out as particularly alternative.

"This okay with you?" Ryan asked quietly as they approached the bar.

"Yeah, it's good."

"What do you want to drink?"

"Do you think they do my version of a Bellini?" Johnny flashed him a grin.

Ryan chuckled. "They probably have peach schnapps and Prosecco, so I can ask?"

"Nah. I'll stick with something a bit less alcoholic tonight. Um...." Johnny leaned over the bar to study the rows of bottles in the fridges. The position made him stick his arse out and Ryan wished he was behind him so he could sneak a proper look at it. "I'll have one of the fruit ciders, the passion fruit and berry one."

"You like your fruity drinks, huh?" Ryan tried not to wrinkle his nose at the thought.

"Yeah. I like cider, and the sweeter the better. The fruit stuff is lush."

When the barman came over, Ryan ordered Johnny's cider and got a pint of bitter for himself. Once they had their drinks they found a small table in a quiet corner.

Johnny slipped off his leather jacket to reveal a bright purple T-shirt with short capped sleeves and a neck that dipped low in the front. It was a thin fabric that clung to his shoulders, which were slender but still wide enough to be unmistakably masculine. He wore a black leather thong necklace with a silver spiral on it that nestled in the little dip between his collarbones. His skin was pale and smooth and Ryan's fingers itched with the urge to touch him.

Ryan was still nervous, so he took a few large swallows of his pint, hoping the alcohol would chill him out a bit.

"Do you really like that stuff, or do you just drink it to

be manly?" Johnny asked, eyeing Ryan over the rim of his glass.

"I guess it's an acquired taste, but I wouldn't drink it if I didn't enjoy it. I'm secure enough in my masculinity that I could drink pink cocktails if I liked them. But beer is nice."

"Would you even drink a pink cocktail with a glittery rainbow umbrella?"

"Even that."

"Hmm." Johnny looked sceptical. "Another time I should take you out drinking to places where you can get those then."

"You already got me drunk on Bellini. I think I've proved to you that I can drink anything."

"Yeah, but look what happened when you drank Bellini." Johnny's grin was wicked. "It made you have gay sex. Who knows what you'd do after pink cocktails with rainbow umbrellas?"

Ryan glanced around to see if anyone was listening to their conversation, but nobody seemed to be. Changing the subject quickly he asked, "So, did you manage to get all your unpacking done?" He picked up his pint again, drinking as Johnny answered.

"Yeah. It didn't take me too long. It's a nice room, bigger than my old one and there's more storage space so it's looking pretty good already. How long have you been living in the house next door?"

"I moved in at the start of my second year, so nearly two years now."

"You doing your finals soon then? Hence all the revising?"

"Yeah. They start in about two weeks." Ryan felt the familiar lurch of dread in the pit of his stomach at the thought. He knew he should do fine. He was a good student and he'd worked consistently hard for three years, but now the moment of truth was so close he couldn't help worrying he was going to fuck up somehow. He took another long swallow from his pint.

"You're drinking quickly," Johnny remarked. He'd barely touched his drink, and Ryan's pint was half-empty. "Are you nervous?"

Surprised by the direct question, Ryan answered honestly. "Yes." He met Johnny's cool, grey gaze. "A bit. Aren't you?"

Johnny shrugged. "Not really. What is there to be nervous about?"

"For you, nothing maybe. But for me this is new."

"Going out for a drink with another guy? Surely you've done that before." Johnny's voice was teasing.

Maybe it was the alcohol on his nearly empty stomach that made Ryan reply bluntly. "Yeah. But I've never done it with a guy I've had sex with." He was careful to speak quietly, so only Johnny would hear him.

There was a pause while their eyes locked, and Johnny's pupils grew larger as they stared at each other. "Yeah, I guess not," he said finally. His lips curved in a mischievous smile. "Well, drink up then. And I'll try and catch up." He lifted his glass and took a few swallows, his throat bobbing enticingly as he did so. Putting his now also half-empty glass back down, he belched, and wiped his mouth with the back of his hand. "Excuse me."

BY THE END of the second drink, Ryan was feeling much more mellow. They'd stuck to safe topics after Ryan's admission of nerves, talking about their housemates, and then moving on to discuss films and TV shows they liked. Johnny rolled his eyes when Ryan mentioned watching football on TV. "You're so predictable."

Ryan shrugged it off, laughing. "What? Loads of guys like football."

"I know. But still. Drinking beer, watching football, wearing manky old trainers and a hoodie out to the pub—"

"Hey, these trainers aren't manky!" Ryan protested. "They're only a few months old."

Johnny shrugged. "Still. You're just so *straight*."

"I am straight—well, mostly," Ryan added quickly as Johnny raised an eyebrow. "And there's no need to make it sound like an insult." His glass was empty again, and Johnny's drink was nearly finished too. "You want to stay here for another drink? Or head off?"

"Head home, or to a different pub?"

Ryan checked his watch, it wasn't even nine o'clock yet, and he was on study leave now so he didn't need to get up early. "I'm up for another drink if you are."

"I'm working early tomorrow, but fuck it. It's not like my job is particularly challenging. As long as I don't go in reeking of booze I'll be fine. Let's go somewhere else though."

They stood, and Johnny slid his black leather jacket over the purple T-shirt. With it on, he looked more like a sexy ninja than a grungy rock chick. Ryan couldn't decide which look he preferred. He couldn't deny his attraction. The casual flirtation when they'd first arrived at the pub had piqued his interest, but since then things had been very platonic between them. He couldn't tell whether they were on the same page or not and he was afraid to ask. Maybe more alcohol would give him the courage to make a move.

SIX

Johnny was encouraged by the way Ryan's gaze raked over him as he zipped up his jacket. He was pretty sure Ryan was interested, even if he wasn't necessarily okay with the fact that he was interested. His conflict was obvious with how nervous he was, and how he'd reacted when Johnny mentioned the word *gay* a bit too loudly in the pub. Straight guys who wanted to bang him annoyed Johnny with their internalised homophobia, but they turned him on too. The idea that he was something forbidden, that they couldn't resist him gave him a thrill; plus knowing what a mindfuck it was for them was weirdly satisfying.

Out in the street, it was dark now and Johnny deliberately walked close enough to Ryan that their elbows brushed occasionally. "Where are we going next?" he asked.

"The White Horse," Ryan replied. "It's another pub that's pretty chilled. Nice for a quiet drink rather than a wild night out."

"Sounds good—not that I'm opposed to wild occasionally."

"Where do you go when you want to party?"

"Troopers usually. They do an LGBT night every Thursday and it's not bad."

"Thursday's a weird night to go out though."

"Nah, it's okay. Means it's mostly full of students, or people who want to pull students. Either way the drinks aren't too expensive and there are plenty of hot, willing guys there."

"So, do you often hook up with random blokes when you go out?" Ryan asked.

"Yeah. Do you?" Johnny nudged him. "Or was I an exception?"

Ryan gave a nervous chuckle. "You were an exception. I hook up with girls sometimes though. But not often on the first night I meet them."

"Yeah, well most girls aren't so into that."

"Hmm." There was a pause, while the tread of their feet marked out the seconds passing. Then Ryan asked, "So, how often do you hook up? And do you ever date people or are you more into one-offs?"

"I dunno. Depends how horny I am, how busy I am, and who I can find to play with. Maybe a couple of times a week? I meet guys on Grindr too sometimes. I'm not looking for anything serious, but it's not all one-offs. Sometimes I do repeats, or even regular for a while till one of us gets bored. I'm not sure it qualifies as dating if you're just meeting to fuck though."

Ryan snorted. "No. I guess not."

"I'm not into relationships. I like to keep things casual." Regular sex with the same person could be fun, but he didn't want commitment or monogamy. He'd never understood that desire to tie yourself down to one person. Not since the one time he'd tried it and had been burned badly.

Never again.

Casual, open arrangements suited him better.

It occurred to Johnny that this situation was out of the norm for him. Going out for a drink with someone he was interested in fucking again wasn't how he normally operated. Usually he'd have asked them directly, but he wasn't sure Ryan would have been receptive without a bit of a warm up. The idea of something regular with Ryan was appealing. He was hot, and he lived next door, and there was a lot to be said for convenience. Johnny could never be bothered to travel too far for sex. He tended to ignore guys on Grindr unless they were an easy walk from where he lived, or were prepared to drive to him. "Why all the questions anyway? You worried you caught something from me —because I play it safe and I test regularly—or are you just generally interested in my sex life?"

"The latter. It's interesting how different it is for guys hooking up with guys instead of girls. It sounds much less complicated."

Johnny shrugged. "Yeah, I suppose. It's certainly easy to get laid as long as you're not too picky."

"Charming!" Ryan laughed. "Good to know you're not fussy."

"Oh shut up. You're hot and you know it."

"You think so?" Ryan stopped. They were outside the pub now, and the light outside lit his face. His boy-next-door good looks were perfectly set off in the warm yellow glow. He grinned at Johnny. "You think I'm hot?"

Johnny moved closer, watching the smug expression on Ryan's face shift into anticipation. Close enough to touch now, Johnny put his hand on Ryan's hip and leaned in to whisper in his ear. "Yeah. You're hot, and you were a good fuck." Then he slid his hand across and grabbed Ryan's crotch hard, making him gasp. "You also have a really nice dick." The pub door burst open and Johnny snatched his hand away and stepped back as a group of people spilled out onto the pavement. "It's your turn to buy the drinks." With that, he led the way into the pub.

At the bar, Ryan's cheeks were flushed and he avoided meeting Johnny's eyes as he ordered for both of them. This pub didn't have fruity cider, much to Johnny's disappointment, so he went with the stuff they had on tap. It wasn't as sweet as the bottles, but it was still pretty good. He picked up his pint as Ryan was paying, "I'll go and find us a table."

Johnny deliberately picked one in a little snug off the side of the bar. There were only two tables in there and the other one was empty. If they were lucky they'd probably get to keep it all to themselves. He put his drink on the table that was tucked around the corner, hidden from view unless someone actually came down the step from the main bar. Waiting until Ryan had spotted him, Johnny slid onto the bench seat that backed onto the wall, leaving plenty of space for Ryan.

When Ryan rounded the corner he hesitated for a moment, so Johnny patted the seat beside him.

Ryan sat, leaving a gap so they weren't touching. He took a gulp of his pint and misjudged it, slopping a little beer down his chin and onto his hoodie. "Bollocks." He wiped his mouth with his hand and dabbed ineffectively at the wet patch on his clothes.

Johnny chuckled. "I thought you played football? I bet you're no good at scoring if you can't even find your own mouth with a pint. You missed a bit. Here...." He caught a few drops of beer on Ryan's chin with his fingertips and sucked them clean, watching as Ryan's pupils expanded, eclipsing some of the blue.

Encouraged, Johnny spread his legs so his knee touched Ryan's. Ryan didn't move away.

"What are you studying again? I forget." Johnny took another sip of his cider. The fruit one had been strong and he hadn't eaten much today, so he was feeling a little buzzed already.

"Chemistry," Ryan said.

"So you're a geeky science-guy?" Johnny grinned. "Do you have to wear a lab coat? Lab coats are hot."

"Sometimes." Ryan grinned back. "And really? You have a thing for lab coats?"

"I like any sort of uniform. And lab coats are what doctors wear, and medical kink is always fun in porn."

"What sort of medical kink?" Ryan frowned. "Not like blood and guts and stuff?"

Johnny laughed. "God no. Definitely not into blood play. Just the whole 'oh hey, sexy doctor, I'm here about a problem with my dick. I can't get hard when I'm with a woman' and then the sexy doctor examines the guy's dick—usually with his mouth—and he realises he doesn't have erectile dysfunction after all."

"Oh yeah. That sounds pretty hot actually." Ryan shifted in his seat, pressing a little closer to Johnny.

"And of course there's always the prostate exam cliché. It's best if the guy going for the exam is an anal virgin and the doctor has to talk him through it. 'Now just bend over, son, this might hurt a little,' and then he puts latex gloves on and lubes up his finger...." Johnny felt his dick getting hard at the thought of it. Maybe Ryan would want to do that to him?

"Fuck. You need to send me some links," Ryan said.

"Yeah, you'd be into that?"

"Maybe."

"Just to watch it? Or to do it with someone?"

Ryan shrugged, gaze fixed on his drink as he picked it up. "Not sure. Maybe both." He took another swallow of his pint.

Johnny put his hand on Ryan's thigh, high up, and squeezed. Leaning in close to Ryan's ear he said quietly, "I'd let you do it to me."

Putting his drink down, Ryan turned to Johnny then. Eyes dark and intense he asked, "What are you looking for—with me?"

"Just to fuck. Like I said earlier. I'm not looking for anything serious. But I like repeats with guys I've had fun with. And I had a lot of fun with you." Ryan stared at him, and Johnny could almost see the cogs turning. He wondered what mental calculations Ryan was struggling with. His sexuality? Whether he wanted something regular? Whether he had time for it with his exams approaching? Maybe all of the above. "But it's no big deal," Johnny added lightly. "If you're not interested that's cool."

"I am interested," Ryan said quickly. "Just...."

"Nervous?"

Ryan nodded.

"Want to get it over with? Our second fuck? Once you've got your dick in me I'm pretty sure you won't be nervous anymore."

"Yeah. That sounds like a good idea. Tonight? Now?"

"Yes," Johnny said. "Let's finish our drinks and go."

"Okay." Ryan's pint was nearly empty anyway, and he drained it in a couple of swallows.

"Someone's keen." Johnny took another mouthful. The cider was fizzy and hard to drink quickly, but he didn't want to waste it.

"I need a piss anyway, so you finish up while I go to the

toilet." Ryan put a heavy hand on Johnny's thigh. He leaned over and kissed Johnny on the cheek. Surprised at the unexpected move from Ryan, Johnny turned and kissed him on the mouth. He tasted of beer, bitter after the sweetness of the cider, and his tongue was hot and insistent. He pulled away before Johnny was ready to give him up. "I'm going to pee."

As Johnny watched Ryan round the corner into the main bar, a rush of impulsiveness hit him like a truck. Taking a few more swigs of his drink for courage, he waited, counting the seconds in his head. Then he left his drink and followed Ryan to the toilet.

Bingo.

Johnny had timed it perfectly. Ryan was washing his hands when Johnny came in, and the gay sex gods were on their side, because there was nobody else in there and the one cubicle stood with its door ajar.

"Hey." Ryan greeted him in surprise. But that was all he managed to say before Johnny grabbed him and hustled him into the cramped cubicle, kicking the door shut, and locking it behind them.

"What—?" Ryan began, but Johnny shut him up by kissing him, hoping that was answer enough. Ryan was tense, his arms braced on the back of the door. He didn't kiss Johnny back at first, and Johnny thought Ryan was going to break away and put a stop to what they were doing. He put his hands on Ryan's arse, pulling him closer and grinding against him, and it was like putting a lit match to crumpled paper. Suddenly Ryan was giving as good as he got, one hand tangling in Johnny's hair as he thrust his tongue into Johnny's mouth. He slipped his other hand into Johnny's unzipped jacket and stroked his torso, mapping out the planes of Johnny's abs and chest.

Johnny wasn't even sure what he'd come in here expecting. He'd given into the impulse to follow Ryan and start something without any plan for what he'd deliver. He got a hand between them to grope Ryan's cock and it was just as big as he'd remembered. The urge to have it inside him was overwhelming, but he didn't think Ryan would want to fuck him in a toilet cubicle, and he didn't have a condom with him anyway. But having it in his mouth would be the next best thing. Taking control, Johnny turned them around, and broke the kiss to reach behind him and slam the toilet seat shut.

"What are you doing?" Ryan's expression was glazed, lips wet and pink from their kisses.

Johnny sat down. Looking up at Ryan with a wicked grin on his face, he hooked his fingers into Ryan's belt loops and pulled until Ryan's crotch was level with his face. "What do you think?"

"We can't. Not here...." But Ryan made no move to stop him as Johnny unbuckled his belt and started to work on his fly.

"We can. We're locked in. Nobody can see us. As long as we're quiet, nobody will know."

Ryan looked around nervously, but the cubicle was one with floor to ceiling walls, so there wouldn't be two telltale pairs of feet visible to anyone outside. There was just a small gap above the door where noise could escape, but Johnny was prepared to risk it. Worst-case scenario they'd get busted and could never drink in this pub again, and there were plenty of other pubs around.

Reaching into Ryan's underwear to free his cock, Johnny found hard flesh waiting for him. Being anxious about getting caught obviously wasn't a turn off. He gripped

Ryan's erection and pumped it a few times, looking up at Ryan and waiting to see how he reacted.

"Fuck," Ryan muttered. Then he took hold of Johnny's head and guided him forward. "Yeah. Suck me."

Johnny took him deep, letting Ryan thrust into his mouth. His hands now free, Johnny undid his fly and tried to work his cock out, but it was trapped. Pulling off just long enough to say, "Hang on, let me...." He half-stood so he could get his jeans and underwear down around his knees and sat again. The lid of the toilet was cold on his arse and he flinched, but Ryan distracted him by shoving his cock back into Johnny's mouth and fucking his face. Johnny started jerking himself off, horny as hell from the whole situation. Ryan taking control, being somewhere public, feeling trapped with his jeans around his legs like restraints. He let Ryan use his mouth, opening his throat to take him deeper. When he gagged, he ignored it, moaning around Ryan's dick as his eyes watered with the effort of taking it.

"Jesus, Johnny," Ryan whispered. "That's so good. Look at me."

Johnny tilted his head back a little and opened his eyes to see Ryan watching him. One hand firmly on the back of Johnny's neck, Ryan touched Johnny's cheek with his other hand, the gentle trail of his fingertips a contrast with the brutal thrust of his cock. Ryan was flushed and breathless, eyes wild. Johnny thought he might come soon, and had a flash of regret that he'd rushed this. Once Ryan came he probably wouldn't want to go back home to fuck. But Johnny couldn't bring himself to stop, like a truck with faulty brakes, the momentum they'd built up was too much and he was powerless to slow things down.

Fate intervened as they heard the outer door to the toilets open. They both froze, Johnny with his mouth still around Ryan's cock as the heavy tread of footsteps echoed on the tiled floor.

The door rattled as someone tried to open it, and gave a *humph* of annoyance at finding it occupied.

Please let him not need a shit, Johnny thought.

Mercifully, the footsteps moved away, followed by the stream of piss hitting a urinal accompanied by a grunt of release and a loud fart. Johnny was glad Ryan's dick was still in his mouth, otherwise he might have laughed. He looked up and met Ryan's panicked expression. His cock was softening rapidly, as was Johnny's, so Johnny let it slip free and grinned reassuringly.

They listened to the rustle and zip, and more footsteps, and then the door opening and closing with a thud.

"Fuck." Ryan moved like lightning, tucking his cock away, and zipping up. Johnny followed suit at a more leisurely pace. It was clear that this little interlude was over.

Ryan opened the cubicle door cautiously, then hurried out and went over to the sinks. "What if that person is sitting near the loos and sees us leave together? He'll know we were both in there."

Johnny shrugged. "So what if he does. He's not gonna say anything is he? But if you're worried, you can leave first and wait outside the pub for me. Then I'll be the one who gets the dirty looks."

"Yeah okay." Ryan still looked worried.

"You going then?"

"Hang on, your eyeliner's running. You might want to fix it." Ryan reached up with his thumb and brushed at the skin under one of Johnny's eyes.

"Oh fuck, yeah. My eyes were streaming from gagging on your cock. I bet I look like Alice Cooper. I'll sort it out and see you outside in minute or so."

"Okay." Ryan squared his shoulders and marched through the door, leaving Johnny alone.

Johnny turned to look in the mirror over the sink. Licking his finger, he wiped away the worst of the smudges. When he was done, he followed Ryan out. Nobody seemed to be looking at him weirdly so he reckoned they'd got away with it.

Outside, he found Ryan waiting under a streetlamp with his hands in his pockets.

"You still wanna fuck?" Johnny asked.

"Yeah. Only somewhere where we won't get interrupted, or arrested."

Johnny chuckled. "Your place or mine, then?"

"Yours," Ryan said quickly. Johnny wasn't surprised. Ryan was still clearly uncomfortable about hooking up with Johnny, so he wouldn't want his housemates seeing them together.

"Let's go then."

SEVEN

Ryan was pretty sure this was a terrible idea.

After what just happened in the toilets, he didn't think that fucking Johnny was going to help get him out of his system. He suspected it would have the exact opposite effect. But right now, Ryan's libido was in the driving seat, putting its foot down, and his rational brain was tied up and locked in the boot. Because damn, he wanted Johnny so badly he couldn't think straight—no pun intended.

They walked quickly and in silence. The silence wasn't exactly comfortable, but it wasn't awkward either. It was filled with sexual tension and an air of purpose as they strode home through the dark streets. Ryan kept his hands shoved in his pockets to stop him doing something crazy like reaching for Johnny's hand, or putting his arm around him. If he was with a girl going back to fuck, he wouldn't have hesitated though. He glanced sideways at Johnny, his fine features intense as he walked, pale hair whipped by the breeze.

"What?" Johnny met his gaze, catching him looking.

"Nothing." Ryan wasn't going to admit where his

thoughts had been. Would Johnny let him hold his hand? Did Ryan actually want to, or did he just think of doing it because it felt natural after what they'd been doing—and what they were going to be doing soon?

"Not having second thoughts?"

"No," Ryan said firmly.

Johnny rewarded him with a grin. "Good."

RYAN WAITED as Johnny unlocked his front door, and followed him inside. His heart was beating hard, and not just because they'd hurried home.

"Wanna go straight up?" Johnny asked.

"Yes."

Ryan was hoping to get up to Johnny's room without meeting anyone, but his luck ran out on the upstairs landing when Ewan and Dev came down from the top floor as Johnny was opening the door to his room.

"Oh!" Ewan said in surprise. "Hey, Johnny. And Ryan. Hi. Fancy meeting you here."

"Hi," Ryan muttered, meeting Ewan's broad grin, and giving him a feeble smile back. "Hi, Dev."

"Hey," Dev said, ducking away from Ryan's gaze. Dev was pretty shy at the best of times and Ryan was grateful for that now.

"Come on, lover boy." Johnny grabbed Ryan's hand and tugged him into his room. "See you later, guys." He closed the door firmly behind them, but Ryan could hear Ewan laughing as he and Dev went downstairs.

"Lover boy. Really?" He raised his eyebrows.

Johnny smirked. "Whatever." He put his hands on Ryan's shoulders and drew him close. Nose-to-nose they stared into each other's eyes and Johnny's breath tickled Ryan's lips.

Transfixed, Ryan held still as Johnny pushed Ryan's jacket off his shoulders, letting it fall to the floor. Then he unzipped Ryan's hoodie and slid that off too. Running his hands over Ryan's chest, he murmured, "I love how muscular you are. The jock thing really does it for me. Lift your arms up." Ryan obliged, and his T-shirt came off next. "God, you're hot." Johnny stroked his shoulders and down over his pecs with hands that were cool from being outdoors. They felt good on Ryan's flushed skin. His nipples hardened under Johnny's touch, tingling as Johnny rubbed them with his fingertips. "Does that feel good? You sensitive there?"

"Yeah," Ryan managed. It came out embarrassingly husky. And when Johnny dipped his head and licked one of his nipples, Ryan couldn't hold in a moan.

Johnny started stroking Ryan's cock through his jeans as he licked and sucked, circling Ryan's nipple with his tongue, and Ryan's legs felt like they were going to give out with the rushing swoop of arousal that flooded him. He clutched at Johnny, frustrated at the lack of bare skin for him to touch. He tried to reach the zip on Johnny's leather jacket but couldn't get to it. "Take your jacket off," he said.

Johnny straightened up, licking his lips. He met Ryan's gaze as he slid the zip down teasingly slowly. He shrugged the black leather off his shoulders and it hit the floor with a heavy thud. The purple T-shirt looked so good on him, bright against his smooth, fair skin. Ryan kissed Johnny again, then worked his way down over his jaw to his neck. Johnny moaned in appreciation and tilted his head back, hands coming up to grab Ryan's hips and pull him flush against him. Ryan trailed open-mouthed kisses over Johnny's warm skin, breathing in the scent of him. There was just the barest hint of stubble against his lips, reminding him that Johnny was a guy—if he could have forgotten with their dicks pressed together.

Pulling away again, Ryan growled. "T-shirt off."

Johnny's lips curved in amusement and he raised his eyebrows. "I like it when you're bossy."

"Yeah? Good." Ryan was okay with being in control. He felt safer that way.

He watched as Johnny stripped off the purple T-shirt in one sinuous movement, his slender torso flexing as he pulled it over his head and tossed it aside. "What do you want to do to me?" Johnny asked.

Ryan swallowed. For the moment he just wanted to look. Johnny was so beautiful, flawless even in the bright overhead light of his room. Footsteps on the landing and the sound of voices reminded Ryan they were in a house full of people. The things he wanted to do to Johnny would probably result in them being pretty noisy if the previous time was anything to go by. "Can you put some music on?" he asked.

"You planning on being loud?"

"I'm planning on making you moan like last time. So unless you want your housemates to hear you...."

Johnny's grin was wicked. "I don't care if they hear."

"Well I do." It wasn't only embarrassment. Johnny's noises were for him, and Ryan didn't want to share.

"Okay." Johnny got out his phone and did something with it, then put it on a docking station on his desk. Music filled the room, something slow and sexy with a heavy beat that Ryan didn't recognise. Perfect music to fuck to. Johnny turned on the lamp by the bed. "Mood lighting too? Wanna turn off the main one?"

Ryan hit the switch, and flipped the lock on the door just in case.

He turned back to see Johnny standing by the bed. Still in his black skinny jeans and boots, a tangle of blond hair falling around his face and skimming his shoulders, he reminded Ryan vividly of the guy in the magazine in the leather trousers.

"Well?" Johnny spread his arms out. "You're in charge."

"Turn around," Ryan said, his throat dry.

Johnny gave him a quizzical look, but he complied. The heavy boots emphasised the length and grace of his legs. His shoulders were wide, and the cut of his shoulder blades was brought into sharp relief by the shadows. The curve of his arse was the only softness to him, and it drew Ryan's gaze like a beacon. He rubbed his cock through his jeans, rock hard at this merging of fantasy and reality. Needing more, he unzipped so he could wrap his hand around himself and stroke properly. Wet with precome already, he didn't want too much stimulation, but he needed something.

"Look at me... over your shoulder."

When Johnny did, his gaze dropped to Ryan's cock. "Fuck. That's hot. But are you going to actually touch me? Or do you just want to look at my arse and jerk off? Because if it's the latter, then can I jerk off too?"

"Oh I'm going to touch you. But I like looking first." Ryan was definitely going to touch. There was no way he was wasting this opportunity. "Bend over the desk."

Johnny obeyed immediately, moving to put his hands on the flat surface. Legs slightly apart, hips tilted, he let his head drop. He didn't speak, but his ribs lifted with each rapid breath as he waited.

Ryan moved in behind him, pressing his cock against that perfect arse as he leaned forward and kissed Johnny's shoulders. Johnny moaned and pushed back against him, the rough denim rubbing Ryan's dick. "Please," he said.

"Please what?"

"Do something. Anything. Touch my dick, my arse, both...."

Ryan grabbed Johnny's arse cheeks in his hands and squeezed. "Like this?"

"Yeah, only with less clothes would be good."

Less clothes sounded good to Ryan too. He reached around and popped open the button on Johnny's jeans and slid the zip down. He eased the fabric over Johnny's arse to reveal skimpy purple briefs. Remembering the pink lace panties, Ryan felt a flash of disappointment, but these still looked good. He worked Johnny's jeans down around his thighs and kissed his shoulders again, grinding his cock insistently against that pert little arse. Reaching around, he rubbed and squeezed Johnny's cock through his underwear, then worked his hand into the waistband to stroke it skin-on-skin. It felt weird having another guy's dick in his hand, familiar, yet not. Johnny was smaller than him, in all dimensions, but he was harder than Ryan ever got. So hard it felt like it would snap if Ryan was too rough with it.

"Feels good," Johnny gasped as Ryan experimented, stroking Johnny harder, letting the head pop through the grip of his fist. He pushed his arse back against Ryan's erection and distracted him. Because while stroking Johnny's cock was more fun than Ryan would have expected, Ryan was way more interested in getting inside his arse.

Letting go of Johnny's cock, Ryan pulled Johnny's briefs down with his jeans. He ran his hands over the backs of his thighs, the fine blond hairs tickling his palms. Then when he dropped to his knees, the sight of Johnny's balls was another reminder of Johnny's masculinity.

Johnny tried to widen his stance, but was trapped by his clothing. He gave a huff of frustration. "Come on."

"What do you want?" Ryan stroked his arse cheeks, which were smoother than his legs. He parted them to see Johnny's hole, the secret furl of it exposed for Ryan's admiration.

"I want you to lick my arse." Johnny thrust his hips back. "I know you want that too."

Unable to wait any more, Ryan gave into his instincts. Burying his face in Johnny's crack, he tongued his hole, burrowing in to find where the texture of his skin changed. He was rewarded with a gasp, so he did it some more.

"Oh yeah." Johnny reached back and slid his fingers into Ryan's hair, holding him where he wanted him. "That's so good."

Losing himself in giving Johnny pleasure, Ryan licked up and down, around in circles, working his tongue in deeper as the sounds Johnny made grew louder. He stroked his own cock at the same time, just enough to keep himself hard but not enough to get close. He wanted to be able to fuck Johnny without coming too quickly after he was done with rimming him.

Johnny's moans got progressively more desperate. "Need more," he finally begged. "Fuck me. Please."

"You got a condom?" Ryan drew back, wiping spit off his face.

"Chest of drawers, top left."

Ryan rummaged in what seemed to be Johnny's underwear drawer. It was an interesting mixture of boxer briefs, briefs, and obviously feminine underwear in a variety of colours. But he didn't find any condoms. "Are you sure?"

"Right at the back."

"Oh yeah." Ryan felt the box with his fingertips.

"There's lube in there too."

After a bit more digging Ryan found it, and also discovered a bright pink dildo of generous proportions. He left that where it was, and brought the lube and a condom.

Johnny was still leaning over the desk. Head down, arse sticking out, he was slowly sliding a finger in and out of his hole.

"Jesus, you look hot like that." Ryan wished he could take a photo so he could remember this forever. "Want me to fuck you here? Over your desk?"

"Yeah. Hurry up."

Ryan chuckled as he tore into the condom wrapper. "I thought I was in charge."

"You are as long as you do it right."

Ryan shoved his jeans down. Not wanting to waste time taking his shoes off, he'd have to manage with them around his knees like Johnny's were. There was something hot about being partly clothed. The desperation of not pausing to get naked was a turn on, like Johnny sucking him in the toilet earlier had been. He rolled the condom onto his cock, then slicked his shaft. "You're going to have to get your finger out of your arse if you want my dick in there."

Johnny let his finger slip free as Ryan moved in close behind him. Rubbing the head of his cock over Johnny's hole a few times, Ryan grinned as Johnny cursed him. "Fucking tease. Get on with it!"

Ryan lined up and pushed. There was resistance for a moment and then blissful tight heat as he slid inside. Now it was Ryan's turn to groan, as Johnny squeezed around him, gripping his cock like a sleek, hot fist. Resisting the urge to start fucking him, Ryan muttered, "This okay? You need a moment?"

"No." Johnny eased forward and pushed back, taking Ryan even deeper. "No. It's good this time."

"You sure?"

"Yes."

Gripping Johnny's hips, Ryan started to fuck him. Johnny groaned, leaning lower over the desk, the muscles in his back tensing as he pressed back to meet each thrust. Ryan already recognised what Johnny sounded like when he was enjoying himself, so he fucked him harder, watching his cock sliding in and out like a piston. Their skin slapped together, and soon sweat began to prickle on Ryan's back with the effort.

Johnny still had both hands braced on the desk, so his dick wasn't getting any stimulation at all. It was hard for Ryan to imagine how it felt good, but Johnny was still moaning and muttering curses and words of appreciation. Ryan was getting close, so he changed his rhythm, slowing to a gentle grind of his hips as he lowered his body over Johnny's. He pressed his chest to Johnny's back, sweat slippery between them, and reached for one of Johnny's hands. Lacing their fingers together, he kissed Johnny's shoulders and the bumps of his spine as he squeezed his arse gently with his free hand. "You love being fucked, don't you?"

"No, it's horrible."

Ryan froze for a second, then realised he was kidding. "Wanker." He slapped Johnny's arse, intending to be playful, but it ended up a little harder than he'd intended.

"Ouch!" Johnny jerked.

"Sorry, sorry." Ryan smoothed his palm over the skin apologetically. "I didn't mean to do it so hard."

"It's okay. I like it. I just wasn't expecting it."

"Yeah?"

"Mmm." Johnny wriggled his arse as Ryan thrust in

deep again. "And to answer your original question. Duh. Yes I love being fucked, Captain Obvious."

Ryan gave him another slap for being cheeky, making him gasp. "Even when you're not stroking your cock?"

"Yeah. Sometimes it's better when I'm not stroking my cock, because then I'm totally focused on my arse and how it feels. But when I want to come, I like both."

"Do you want to come?" Ryan reached around to feel Johnny's cock. He was hard and wet as Ryan stroked him slowly, trying to time it with the thrust of his dick in Johnny's arse.

"Yeah," Johnny said breathlessly. "And I'm going to do it really soon if you keep doing that."

"Cool." Ryan carried on, his own climax at bay while he concentrated on what he was doing to Johnny. He adjusted his grip slightly, so he could stroke faster.

"Oh yes. Don't stop!" Johnny pushed back against Ryan's cock, meeting each thrust, and fucking into Ryan's fist as he moved forward again. "Yeah. Oh fuck."

Hot come spilled over Ryan's hand as Johnny stilled, moaning and clenching around Ryan's dick. Then another jet of come splattered onto the desk. Releasing Johnny's cock, Ryan got both hands on his hips and started to fuck him again. "This okay?" he asked, unsure if it would still feel good for Johnny now he'd come.

"Yeah. You going to come soon?"

"Yes." Ryan looked down, and the sight of his cock sliding into Johnny's hole pushed him closer. He gave a breathless chuckle. "I left a handprint on your arse when I slapped you." The mark was clear, pink on Johnny's pale skin.

"How does it look?"

"It looks hot." Ryan fucked him harder. "Would look even better with my come all over you."

"Do it," Johnny said.

"You sure? It'll be messy."

"I've just come all over my desk. I think we're past worrying about mess."

"Yeah. I guess so." Ryan drove his cock in deep a few more times, getting himself right to the brink, and then he pulled out. He stripped the condom off frantically and wrapped his hand around his dick, groaning as he began to stroke.

"Yeah, come on." Johnny reached back; gripping his arse cheeks and holding them open so Ryan could see his hole, shiny with lube. Johnny dipped two fingers in, pumping them in and out. The sight of that tipped Ryan over the edge and he came with a groan. The first spurt hit Johnny's crack and the second shot over his back, leaving white streaks up as far as his shoulders.

"Don't get it in my hair!" Johnny said.

Ryan laughed. "Sorry. I meant to aim lower, but I think I missed it." He squeezed out the last few drops with his fingers and rubbed it over the pink marks from his hand.

"You're dirty," Johnny said, looking over his shoulder with a grin. "I like it."

"You're the one who's dirty. I think you need a shower."

"Pass me something to mop up with."

Looking around the room, Ryan couldn't see anything useful, like tissues. "Um... anything in particular?"

"My T-shirt will do."

Ryan pulled up his trousers and underwear so he could move without falling over and went to get Johnny's T-shirt from the floor. On his way back he paused to admire Johnny again.

Leaning forward over the desk, black jeans around his ankles, boots still on, covered in Ryan's come, he made quite a sight. If Ryan hadn't just come he'd have got hard looking at him.

"Dude, come on. My legs are knackered. I need to lie down."

"Can I take a photo of you like that?" Ryan blurted out.

Johnny turned to meet his gaze, amusement on his face. "This do it for you?"

"Yeah," Ryan admitted. "You look amazing."

"Okay then, but don't get my face in it. And I want to see it. If I don't like it, you have to delete the pic."

Ryan got his phone out of his pocket and took a few from different angles. He made sure that Johnny's face wasn't visible. When he was done, he wiped the come off Johnny's back and arse with the T-shirt, and then mopped up Johnny's mess on the desk. "Um... I think you came on your bank statement."

"Never mind," Johnny said, straightening up. "That might make the state of my bank account more exciting." He pulled his underwear and jeans up, and sat on the edge of the bed to take off his boots. When he was done he lay back with a groan. "Damn. My legs nearly gave out while you were fucking me. I'm knackered now." He patted the bed beside him. "Come here and show me your spank bank pics then, so I can veto them if my bum looks big."

Ryan toed off his trainers and went to lie beside him. He scrolled through the pics and Johnny made approving noises.

"Yeah okay, you can keep them. I do look pretty hot like that."

"You look amazing," Ryan said, closing his phone.

"Are you going to jerk off looking at them?" Johnny asked.

"Probably."

Johnny smiled, like a satisfied cat. "That's hot. Send me a photo when you do." He moved closer and ran a hand down Ryan's chest to his stomach. Leaving it there, he leaned over and kissed Ryan on the lips.

Surprised by the affectionate gesture, Ryan hesitated a moment before kissing him back. A strand of Johnny's hair tickled his face, so he reached up and tucked it behind Johnny's ear.

Johnny eventually drew away and lay back with his head on Ryan's shoulder. "So.... How do you feel about hooking up again sometime? I'd be up for something regular if you were." Johnny's voice was casual, but his arm over Ryan's torso felt tense.

Ryan's head reeled at the question. He'd come out tonight half-hoping that this second hook up wouldn't be as good as the first. Then it would have been easy to move on and forget about Johnny. Only it hadn't panned out that way. This time had been just as good as the first, maybe even better. And now he had photos of Johnny's arse on his phone that he was definitely going to be using as wank fodder—probably for the rest of his life. It would be crazy not to say yes if the real thing was on offer, wouldn't it?

"Um... what do you mean by something regular?"

"No strings," Johnny said quickly. "Just like a friends-with-benefits kind of deal. The chemistry between us is great, and living next door to each other is very convenient. Seems like a shame to waste that opportunity."

The idea definitely had its merits. Although Ryan wasn't sure whether living next door to Johnny, the potential for complications would outweigh the convenience. But as long as they went into this with clear boundaries it should be okay. "Yeah. I guess we could give it a try. As long as we're clear about what we're doing. What does no strings mean to you?"

"No commitment, no expectations. We're both free to see other people, but we meet up when it's mutually convenient and we're in the mood for sex."

That sounded manageable. Not that Ryan had the time or inclination to pursue other people at the moment when he was supposed to be focused on revising for his finals. But having Johnny to let off steam with would be perfect. Regular sex was a good stress relief and being able to do that without the hassle of a relationship was ideal. "Okay. That sounds good."

"Cool." Johnny patted Ryan's stomach. "Right. I'm going to kick you out now so I can shower. You okay to let yourself out?"

"Of course."

Ryan dressed quickly, and gave Johnny a quick kiss before leaving. "So, text me I guess? Or I'll text you. Not sure how often you were thinking we'd meet."

"Tuesday evening any good for you?"

"Yeah, Tuesday works." It was only two days away, but Ryan was already eager for more.

"Okay. We'll sort something out for then."

EIGHT

Johnny didn't realise he was humming until Simon, one of his co-workers, told him to stop.

"Seriously, Johnny. It's nice to see you in such a good mood, but it's driving me crazy. What are you even humming anyway?"

Johnny paused in the middle of unpacking the new stock that had just arrived, replaying the song that was stuck in his head so he could work out what it was. "'Rude Boy,' by Rihanna." He snorted. "That song's all about a guy with a big dick isn't it? It's funny how the subconscious works."

Simon laughed. "Oh! No wonder you're in such a good mood. Was he a good fuck as well?"

"Oh hell yes," Johnny said dreamily.

"A one-off? Or are you seeing him again?"

"Hopefully a regular." Johnny put another shirt on a hanger and added it to the rail.

"Lucky you. Do you think it might turn into something serious?" Simon was a romantic, always looking for boyfriends more than hook ups, with limited success.

"I'm not looking for serious. We've been through this,

Si." Johnny enjoyed being young free and—if not necessarily always entirely single—safe from having unrealistic expectations. The one time he'd tried being monogamous it hadn't ended well, and not because of Johnny. The memory of seeing the texts on Craig's phone, the painful evidence that he was fucking around behind Johnny's back, still made him feel sick when he thought about it.

"Well one day you might meet someone who makes you change your mind."

"Yeah, well it won't be this guy." Johnny knew that eventually he might connect with someone who would make him take that risk again, but it was still hard to imagine, even four years later.

"What makes you say that?"

"I think he's more into women than men really. He just likes fucking me."

"Oh, one of those guys. You should steer clear, Johnny, they always leave you feeling like crap."

"They leave *you* feeling like crap because you go in hoping you'll be the one who'll turn them with the magic power of your arse. Surely by now you should have learned that trying to snare guys who call themselves straight even though they're on Grindr is a recipe for disaster. Those guys are never going to leave their wives or girlfriends for you. They just want easy sex on the side. And this guy, Ryan, is one of those; it's only a bit of fun. I'm not looking for more than sex anyway, so it doesn't matter to me that he's never going to want to put a ring on it. The only type of relationship we're ever going to have is a mutually beneficial sexual one, and I'm okay with that."

Johnny shook out another shirt, snapping it to get the creases out before hanging it up with the others.

"If you say so." Simon added some folded jeans to his pile.

"What's that supposed to mean?"

"You've been walking around with a smile on your face all shift. And humming to yourself."

Rolling his eyes, Johnny said, "Good sex will do that to a person. It doesn't mean anything else."

"Hmm." Simon started cutting the tape on the next box.

Johnny ignored him. Just because Simon always ended up falling for the guys he was fucking didn't mean Johnny would. He'd had regular fuck buddies before and it had worked out fine. Sex was sex. Feelings didn't have to come into it. He let his mind drift back to yesterday again, a smile creeping over his face as he remembered bending over his desk for Ryan. Yeah. Ryan was going to be fun to play with.

BY THE TIME he finished work on Tuesday, Johnny still hadn't heard anything from Ryan.

He'd been waiting for Ryan to contact him because he felt as if it was Ryan's turn to initiate something. Johnny had been the one to ask him out, and suggest regular hook ups. It seemed appropriate to back off a little now and let Ryan be the one to take the next step. But as he walked home from the town centre, his fingers itched to send a message. He was horny from thinking about Ryan all day and getting fucked would be way more interesting than going home and jerking off.

Hopeful that Ryan would be in touch about meeting later, Johnny made himself some dinner as soon as he got back. If Ryan messaged, then he'd shower before seeing him. He didn't want to jinx it by douching now. Sod's law said that if he cleaned his arse before the arrangement was confirmed, Ryan would stand him up.

Jez and Mac were in the kitchen, arguing over something they were cooking. "No, you put too much chilli powder in it last time, remember? Just use one spoonful or it will blow our heads off," Jez was saying.

"You're a lightweight," Mac said.

"I'm fucking not!"

"Yeah you are." But Mac only put one spoonful in the pan.

"God you two sound like my mum and dad, except with more swearing," Johnny said. "Hi guys."

"Oh hey, Johnny." Mac turned and gave him a smile.

"Hi, Johnny. How's life?"

"Not bad thanks. Work was boring, but it always is."

Johnny didn't like his job, but he didn't hate it enough to be motivated to do anything different. He'd worked at Top Man ever since he dropped out of uni and it gave him a regular income but wasn't exactly intellectually challenging. At some point he needed to sort his life out and work out what he wanted to do instead of working in retail, but it suited him for now. It was relatively stress free apart from the odd shitty customer, and at least he didn't have to bring any work home with him.

Johnny put a pan of water on and got out pasta. He couldn't be bothered to cook anything from scratch, but he had a jar of sauce he could use.

"Have you got much work to do tonight?" Jez asked Mac.

"Yeah. Loads."

Mac was doing teacher training and was up to his eyeballs in marking most evenings, and Jez often ended up dealing with emails and admin from his conservation job when his working day was supposed to be over. At least they seemed to enjoy what they did though, even if it took up a lot of their time. It must be nice doing something you cared about.

Johnny pondered this as he cooked, and found himself wondering what Ryan's career plans were. He remembered he was studying Chemistry, but the conversation had spun off before Johnny had asked what he wanted to do after he graduated. His brain snagged on the memory of the medical kink conversation, and he smirked as he imagined Ryan in a white coat with a stethoscope around his neck. Yeah, that would be hot.

With perfect timing, Johnny's phone buzzed in his pocket. He stopped stirring his pasta sauce and got his phone out to see a message from Ryan:

Still wanna hook up this evening?

Johnny resisted the urge to do a happy dance because he didn't want to attract Jez and Mac's attention. Dev was the only one who'd seen Ryan on Sunday, and he hadn't said anything about it to anyone as far as Johnny was aware. The rest of his housemates were bound to notice eventually if Ryan kept coming and going—*or coming and coming*, Johnny smirked to himself. But he'd rather be as discreet about this as possible, so Ryan wouldn't get freaked out and bail.

Yeah, he replied. Then added: *My place again?*

Yes, what time?

Eight?

That would give Johnny plenty of time to shower, and maybe tidy up his room a little too. *Perfect. See you then,* he sent back, then put his phone away assuming they were done.

It buzzed again as he was draining his pasta. Johnny

served up his food and carried it through to the living room before checking the message this time. It was another one from Ryan:

What do you want to do tonight?

Johnny frowned, and then typed back: *I assumed we were just hooking up. Not going out anywhere. That okay with you?*

There was a short pause before Ryan's reply came: *Yeah that's not what I meant. But was there anything in particular you'd like to do with me?*

I'm happy to make it up as we go, Johnny typed. *Why? Is there something you want to try?*

This time the reply was fast: *I want to see you in those pink knickers.*

Johnny hesitated, unsure how to respond. Cross-dressing was something he did for himself, because he liked how he looked in women's underwear, and how it felt. It wasn't particularly a sexual thing, and definitely wasn't something he'd ever done for another guy. A flush crawled over his skin as he imagined wearing them for Ryan, how it would make him feel.

A little kinky, a lot submissive.

He liked the idea, and he was getting hard so his dick definitely liked the idea. But he wasn't sure how he felt about Ryan asking for it. Johnny's gut feeling was that Ryan was uncomfortable with his bisexuality, so maybe feminising Johnny was a way of making himself feel better about having sex with him? Johnny might not be the most masculine guy on the planet, but he *was* a guy, and he wanted Ryan to own that when he was fucking him.

Another message appeared:

Is that a no? Sorry if I overstepped. Only I bet you look really good in them.

It's okay, Johnny typed. Then he made up his mind to give it a try; he could always bail if it felt weird. So he added: *and yeah. I'll wear them if you'll wear the lab coat for me sometime* :)

Deal :) Ryan sent back.

JOHNNY'S VEINS pulsed with nervous anticipation as he tidied his room ready for later. He put away some clothes that were strewn around, and tidied his desk in case Ryan wanted to fuck him over it again. Once his room was respectable, he went to brush his teeth, shower, and get his arse squeaky clean. He looked in the mirror while he waited for the water to run hot, and considered shaving, but decided to leave two days' worth of stubble on his chin and jawline. It was quite visible because his natural colour was brown—not the bright, dyed blond of his hair—so it was enough to be clearly masculine.

After his shower, he put on sweatpants before blow-drying his hair. That done, he put a little serum on it to stop it from frizzing, and then smudged some kohl around his eyes as usual and smeared some clear gloss onto his lips. Heart thumping, he rifled through his underwear drawer until he found the pink lace panties. He had a few different pairs of women's knickers, but as Ryan had requested these ones Johnny stepped into them and slid them up. They weren't designed for people with dangly bits, but they were stretchy enough to be reasonably comfortable over his junk. He adjusted himself until they felt okay and then opened the wardrobe to look at himself in the mirror on the inside of the door.

From the front they looked odd. His balls were a bit squashed, and his dick was visible through the lace. Johnny had seen websites where you could order lace underwear that was designed for people with penises, but they tended to be expensive. Plus wearing something that was intended for women was part of the thrill for him. He turned and looked over his shoulder at the reflection of his bum.

Oh yeah.

The back view more than made up for how weird his dick looked. The line of the panties cut across his arse cheeks at exactly the right angle, leaving the pale curves of his buttocks visible in stark contrast to the hot-pink lace.

Satisfied that Ryan was going to approve, Johnny put on a pair of jeans—black as usual—and a deliberately masculine high-necked grey T-shirt. He liked the contrast of the pink lace hidden beneath the monochrome, and he hoped Ryan would appreciate it too. He left his feet bare; he'd be getting undressed soon enough and it was quite warm in his room.

The doorbell rang just before eight, taking Johnny by surprise. He hurried down to answer it, hoping to beat his housemates there. But he was too slow. As he came down the stairs he heard Jez say, "Oh. Hi, Ryan. What's up?"

"I'm here to see Johnny," Ryan said.

Johnny called, "On my way." He descended to see Ryan standing awkwardly in the doorway. "Hey, Ryan." Ryan glanced up at the sound of Johnny's voice and his eyes widened as he stared, taking in Johnny's appearance. His obvious admiration sent a thrill through Johnny. "Jez. You gonna let him in, or leave him on the doorstep?"

"Oh, yeah, sorry, man. Come in." Jez stood aside to let Ryan past. He gave Johnny a knowing look and raised his eyebrows.

Johnny ignored him. "Come on up," he said to Ryan.

On the upstairs landing, Johnny paused and said,

"Sorry. I should have asked you if you wanted a drink or anything."

"I don't," Ryan said.

Johnny let them into his room and shut the door behind them.

"So. What *do* you want?" Johnny raised his eyebrows and gave him a suggestive smile.

"You," Ryan said simply.

"That's the general idea."

"You look gorgeous." Ryan moved closer and put a hand on Johnny's cheek, studying him. "So... pretty. Is it okay to call you pretty?"

"Yeah." Johnny met his gaze. "I like it." It wasn't the first time a guy had used that word to describe him. It made him feel good.

"So. Are you wearing them?" Ryan's gaze dropped to Johnny's crotch, as if staring hard enough would give him X-ray vision.

"Why don't you find out?"

Ryan put his hands on Johnny's waist, tugging him as he kissed him. He started slow and sensual, but as Johnny kissed him back the kiss got deeper and more forceful. Ryan slid his hands around to Johnny's arse as Johnny cupped his face, stroking his thumbs over Ryan's stubble. Ryan worked a hand under the waistband of Johnny's jeans and slid it down until his fingers touched the lace. He hummed his appreciation and broke away from Johnny's mouth to kiss his neck. "I can't wait to see how they look," he muttered between kisses. "You have such a gorgeous arse." He squeezed the arse in question as he said it, pulling Johnny closer, and grinding his erection against Johnny's rapidly hardening bulge.

Then he pulled away, leaving Johnny breathless and

flushed as Ryan reached down to undo Johnny's jeans. He left the fly open but made no move to push them down. Stepping back, Ryan said, "Take your T-shirt off."

Johnny obeyed, exposing his torso to Ryan's hungry gaze. "And now?"

Ryan lifted a finger in the air and twirled it. "Turn around."

Johnny turned, waiting to see what Ryan would ask him to do next. But there were no more instructions. Instead, Ryan came up behind him and pushed the hair away from Johnny's neck and shoulders to kiss the skin. He pressed his crotch against Johnny's arse so Johnny could feel how hard he was. The ticklish kisses on his neck were driving him crazy, but Ryan was in charge. Johnny instinctively knew that he had to be patient.

"I think you should put some music on," Ryan said quietly, his breath warm as he spoke between kisses.

"Yeah, okay." But Johnny couldn't tear himself away.

Ryan put his hands on Johnny's hips and gave him a gentle push towards the desk. "Go on."

"You gonna make me moan again?" Johnny asked as he put his phone in the docking station and chose a suitable playlist to drown out the sex noises.

Ryan chuckled. "I hope so." He moved in close behind Johnny again, stroking his arse through the denim. Then as Johnny pressed play and music started to pour out of the speakers, Ryan tugged Johnny's jeans down, kneeling as he did so. "Lift up." He tapped Johnny's ankle, and tugged on the heel of his jeans to free his foot. "And the other one."

Jeans gone, Johnny stayed where he was, lace-clad arse tilted invitingly. "What do you think, then?" With him nearly naked, and Ryan still fully clothed he felt exposed, slutty—in a good way— and sexy as hell.

"Hot. As. Fuck." Ryan punctuated the words with a kiss on each arse cheek and a final one over his crack. He ran his hands up Johnny's thighs with a light touch, making Johnny shiver. "Spread your legs." As Johnny did so, he reached through to palm Johnny's balls, then higher to where his cock was hard, trapped in the pink lace. He rubbed it and Johnny pressed into his hand, encouraged that Ryan was touching his cock. It helped eliminate his earlier fears about Ryan's motives.

"Do you like stroking my dick?" Johnny asked. "Does it turn you on?"

"Yeah," Ryan said. "It's hot, because when you're hard I know you want me. That's sexy. I like how obvious it is compared to girls."

"But you like me wearing lace," Johnny persisted, wanting to make sense of Ryan's attraction to him. "Even though I'm a guy."

"I like the contrast. It's hot. I used to like it when my ex-girlfriend wore my boxer briefs too. There's something sexy about it. I don't know why." His hand was still on Johnny's cock. "Turn around."

Johnny turned, leaning on the desk, and gripping the edge with his hands as Ryan studied him slowly. His gaze raked down from Johnny's face and over his torso to rest on the obscene bulge of his cock. The see-through lace left very little to the imagination.

Ryan unzipped his jeans and got his dick out. Johnny was glad to see he was hard too.

"You like how they look from the front as well?" Johnny canted his hips, pushing his crotch closer to Ryan's face.

Ryan swallowed, stroking his dick slowly, and then nodded. "Yeah." His voice came out a little husky. He ran his free hand over Johnny's cock, feeling out the shape of him, teasing the head with his fingertips where precome was leaking through the fabric. He moved his face closer and kissed the curve of Johnny's balls.

Surprised by this development, Johnny held still as Ryan slowly slid his mouth up Johnny's shaft, lips parted, breath hot. When he reached the head he opened his mouth. Warm wetness made Johnny gasp as Ryan used his tongue. "Can you taste me?" Johnny asked.

His mouth still on Johnny's cock through the lace, Ryan looked up and nodded.

"You like it?"

Ryan nodded again and mouthed Johnny's cockhead, the sensation of his tongue through the fabric a frustrating tease. Johnny groaned and brought his hands up, threading his fingers in Ryan's hair. With any other guy he'd be getting his cock out and asking for it to be sucked, but he didn't want to push Ryan too far. When Johnny had tried that with bi-curious guys before he hadn't always got a good response, and it was always a boner killer if they flatly refused. Not everyone was a huge fan of dick sucking, even some gay guys weren't particularly into it, but it was never fun to be faced with obvious distaste at the suggestion. Johnny held back, letting Ryan do his thing.

Ryan's thing was apparently driving Johnny completely fucking crazy by teasing him through the panties. He did everything apart from suck. He nuzzled, he licked, he made humming sounds of pleasure. The more he did it, the harder it was for Johnny not to beg Ryan to blow him. Surely that was where this was heading? These weren't the actions of a guy who was scared of having a cock in his mouth. Ryan was still hard too, stroking himself as he teased Johnny.

Finally Johnny's patience was rewarded; Ryan hooked his fingers in the lace and tugged them down slowly, letting

Johnny's cock pop free. He tucked the lace under Johnny's balls and took Johnny's dick in his hand. Pumping it slowly, with the head just an inch away from his lips, Ryan looked up at Johnny. "You want me to suck you?"

Johnny was too far gone for sarcasm. "Yes." He tightened his fingers in Ryan's hair. "If you want."

There was a flash of uncertainty on Ryan's face. "I've never done it before. I might be crap at it."

"I'm okay with being your guinea pig. Seriously Ryan, you can't go too far wrong. Lick, suck, you don't have to take it deep. And you must know what feels good from being on the receiving end. If you don't like doing it, just stop and lick my arse instead. We both know you're good at that."

Ryan grinned. "Yeah. Okay, that's a good plan B."

"Or that's plan A and this is plan B. A for arse, B for blowjob. Or maybe this should be plan D for dick, or C for cock...." Johnny realised he was babbling, while Ryan was still stroking his dick and looking at Johnny as if he was batshit crazy. He probably was, Ryan had turned his brain to mush. "Sorry. Sometimes I forget to stop talking when I'm nervous."

"You're nervous? I'm the one about to suck dick for the first time."

"Yeah. Good point. Okay, I'll shut up, and you can get it over with. Go for it." He let go of Ryan's hair, wanting him to feel safe to do this in his own time with no pressure. Instead he gripped the edge of the desk and waited.

NINE

Ryan eyed Johnny's cock, stroking it once more with his hand while he plucked up his courage, then took the head in his mouth and sucked experimentally. It really was hard to get a blowjob wrong, unless teeth were involved, or so he hoped. Ryan glanced up to gauge Johnny's reaction.

"That's good. You okay?" Johnny smiled down at him.

"Mmm." Ryan took a little more, swirling his tongue around as he carried on jerking the base with his hand. It was weird, because it didn't feel as strange as he'd expected. Once he'd pushed himself over the mental barrier of having another guy's dick in his mouth, physically it was way less intimidating than he'd expected. Johnny didn't taste of anything much, just clean skin. It was a little like sucking on a finger or thumb, only bigger, and the skin was softer.

"Fuck," Johnny muttered. "That feels great."

Meeting his gaze again, Ryan tried to smile, and realised it was impossible with a cock in his mouth. Then he closed his eyes and took Johnny deep. He was glad Johnny's cock was a non-intimidating size because Ryan was able to take it all, until his nose was in Johnny's neatly trimmed pubes.

Feeling pretty smug as Johnny gasped, Ryan reckoned he was doing all right for his first time giving a blowjob.

Johnny moaned, fingers gripping the desk as Ryan slowly slid his mouth up and back down, then did the same again. With each pass Ryan got more confident, sucking harder, and using his tongue on the underside. "Oh Jesus. That's so good."

Pulling off, Ryan replaced his mouth with his fist again as he said, "It's easier than I thought. Or maybe I'm just a natural."

"A natural cocksucker?" Johnny grinned. He cupped Ryan's cheek with one hand and ran his thumb over Ryan's lower lip. "It could just be beginner's luck. I think you'd better try again to make sure... Oh, fuck yeah—" his words turned into a whimper as Ryan sucked him deep again. He put both hands on Ryan's head, gently, and Ryan found he liked the sensation of Johnny guiding him.

Ryan started to stroke his own cock, which had softened due to nerves and the need to concentrate on pleasing Johnny. Now he was getting into his stride, he started to lengthen and thicken again, the sensation of his hand and the sounds Johnny was making teasing him back to hardness.

Suddenly Johnny said, "Ryan. I'm going to come if you carry on doing that."

Pausing for a moment, Ryan considered his options. Then he carried on sucking, hoping Johnny would get the hint. Ryan didn't want to stop; now he'd started this he wanted to see it through. He just hoped he'd be able to swallow because there wasn't anywhere obvious he could spit it out.

"You want me to come in your mouth?" Johnny asked, voice strained.

"Mmhmm," Ryan said around his mouthful of dick. He sucked Johnny harder and faster, stroking and squeezing Johnny's balls as he did so.

"Oh yeah," Johnny encouraged him. "That's perfect. Keep going like that...." He began to thrust into Ryan's mouth, his fingers tightening in Ryan's hair. Ryan took it, and made his own noises of pleasure and approval as Johnny fucked his mouth. The whole experience was turning him on way more than he had expected.

Johnny clutched Ryan's hair so hard it hurt. "Yeah. I'm coming!" Warm salt exploded on Ryan's tongue. He stilled, holding Johnny's cock in his mouth as he pulsed a few more times, his breathing ragged, and body tense.

When he judged Johnny was done, Ryan pulled off, and then swallowed with a wince. He wrinkled his nose. "Yeah that doesn't taste great, does it? Why haven't we evolved better tasting jizz yet?"

Johnny laughed breathlessly. "You're a scientist. Surely you can see that delicious ejaculate wouldn't be in the best interests of a species from an evolutionary point of view."

"Huh. I guess not."

"There's water by the bed if you want to rinse."

"No. I'm okay." Ryan stood. "I'd rather kiss you, then you can share it."

"I don't mind the taste." Johnny reeled Ryan in with a hand around the back of his neck. He kissed him deep, and Ryan wondered whether Johnny could taste his come.

"Not even when it's yours?"

"Especially when it's mine, and it's in someone else's mouth. I think it's hot." Johnny kissed him again. Ryan's erection bumped against Johnny's softening dick, and Johnny took it in his hand and tugged on it a few times. "Seems like I'm not the only one who thinks it's hot. Did you like having my cock in your mouth, and tasting my come?"

"I liked sucking you," Ryan admitted. "More than I thought I would. Not sure about the come in my mouth though, I think 'liked' is a bit strong, more... tolerated."

"It was hot for me. Especially because I know it was your first time." Johnny stroked Ryan's cock more insistently. "So. How do you want to come? Want me to blow you too? Or do you want to fuck me?"

"I want to fuck you," Ryan said immediately. Much as he loved Johnny's mouth on him, he wanted his cock in Johnny's perfect arse again.

"Where do you want me this time?"

"Can we do it doggy? And can you keep these on?" Ryan plucked at Johnny's lacy shorts that were still tugged down just enough that Ryan had been able to get to his cock. He slid a hand around to squeeze Johnny's arse, slipping his fingers into the crack.

"Yes." Johnny smiled. "I'm glad you like them on me."

"I love them." Ryan pulled them back up, tucking Johnny's dick inside. "Now get on the bed and show me how good they look again."

Johnny turned and crawled onto the mattress. He went down onto his elbows, the curve of his back emphasising his butt as he spread his thighs. The bulge of his balls was subtle in the snug lace, but enough to remind Ryan who he was about to fuck. "Lube and a condom?" he asked.

"Same place as last time."

Ryan went to Johnny's underwear drawer again. At some point he'd like a chance to look through it properly, but now getting himself gloved up ready to fuck was more of a priority. He found the lube and a condom and tossed them down on the bed before stripping out of his clothes.

Climbing up behind Johnny, he rolled the condom on, then pulled the pink lace down just enough to give him access to Johnny's hole. He squeezed Johnny's arse, kissing each cheek before slicking his fingers and sliding two carefully into Johnny. Johnny moaned and pushed back on them, so Ryan stopped being so gentle and fucked Johnny steadily with them for a moment.

"I'm ready for your cock," Johnny said. "Go for it."

"Are you going to come again?" Ryan asked, withdrawing his fingers, and lining up his cock at Johnny's hole.

"No. It's too soon. But I want you anyway. I want you to come while you fuck me."

"Fuck." Ryan gasped at the feeling as he pushed inside. "That can definitely be arranged. God. You feel amazing."

He tried to go slowly at first, wanting it to last a little while. But with Johnny moaning and encouraging him, the urge to lose himself was too much. Ryan fucked Johnny faster and faster, breathless and sweating as he slammed into him.

There was a pause in the music as the track changed, and Ryan was briefly aware of the sound of his grunts, the creaking of the bed, and the loud moans knocked out of Johnny with every thrust. He hoped the music was doing a good enough job of covering the racket as it restarted. Pushing his momentary self-consciousness aside, Ryan went back to focusing on the physical as the pleasure built.

"You going to come soon?" Johnny asked.

"Yeah," Ryan managed.

"Tell me when. I want to see if I can feel it."

"'Kay." Ryan slammed into him, harder, harder... and, "Oh fuck yeah. Gonna come." A last few erratic thrusts and Ryan stilled, coming with a harsh groan in an orgasm that seemed to last longer than usual.

"Oh Jesus, that's hot," Johnny said.

"Could you feel it? Even with a condom?"

"Yeah."

Ryan eased himself out of Johnny and dealt with the condom, while Johnny flopped onto his back and rearranged his underwear. He stretched luxuriously. "Damn that was good. The perfect way to end a long work day."

Standing uncertainly at the foot of the bed, Ryan wasn't sure what to do now. With him still naked, and Johnny in nothing but the lacy shorts, he wasn't sure he should get back onto the bed. Last time he'd hung around for a little while, but they'd had clothes on. "Yeah," he said. "I've been revising all day and I needed a break."

Their eyes met and Johnny's expression was hard to read. "Wanna stick around for a bit?" he said casually. "Round two later if you're up for it? Or do you need to head off?"

"Uh. I should probably go." The thought of a second round was appealing, but what would they do in the interim? This was supposed to be a casual, sex-only arrangement, and Ryan wasn't sure how spending a longer evening together would fit with that. "Get back and do another couple of hours' work before bed." Actually he was probably done with studying for the day now, but it gave him an excuse to leave without sounding dismissive. He turned away and started to put his clothes back on.

"Okay. No worries." Johnny got up and shed the panties, pulling on a pair of sweatpants instead.

The silence felt awkward as Ryan dressed. All the intimacy of the sexual act chased away by reality now the high of orgasm had faded. It was weird how you could lose yourself in someone for that short space of time, feel that sense of intense connection based purely on the physical. Then when it passed you realised you were still relative strangers. Ryan felt an ache that was almost like a sense of loss.

"Do you want to meet again soon?" he asked hopefully.

"Yeah, sure. When suits you?"

"Thursday evening?" That was forty-eight hours away. Ryan was starting to feel worryingly addicted to sex with Johnny but he thought he could wait that long. At least he had the photos on his phone to keep him and his right hand company in the meantime. He'd made good use of them yesterday.

"I'm working late on Thursday. I could do tomorrow instead if that's not too soon? Not getting bored of me yet?" Johnny's lips curved in a teasing smile.

Ryan's heart leapt at the thought of seeing Johnny again so soon. "No. Tomorrow sounds good."

"Same time?"

"Sure."

Johnny picked up a towel. "Let yourself out. I'm going to wash off the lube. See you tomorrow." He gave Ryan a kiss on the cheek and they left his room together.

Ryan hurried downstairs, relieved when he managed to get out without meeting anyone. Out in the street he paused, taking a deep breath of the cool evening air. The sky was clear and stars pricked bright holes in the blackness. He wondered what would have happened if he'd hung around for longer. Would they have lain in bed together, exchanged kisses while they got horny again? Watched TV together? Talked? Part of him wished he'd stayed to find out. But it was probably better this way.

Meet, fuck, and leave.

This arrangement was only supposed to be about sex and it was better to keep the boundaries nice and clear. The sex had been amazing. Ryan's body was still buzzing with it. So why did he feel faintly unsatisfied?

RYAN WAS STILL in a weird mood the next day. He woke early feeling anxious and as his brain came into focus, his worries were split between pre-exam nerves and wondering whether this thing with Johnny was a good idea or not. The exam anxiety was more easily tackled, so he tried to push aside all thoughts of Johnny and focus on revising.

In a house full of third year students, tensions were running high with exams less than two weeks away. They all had different routines and preferences when it came to their study habits. Some of them preferred to work in the daytime where others were night owls. Some got out of the house to study for a change of scenery, others tended to work from home.

Ryan usually did his studying at home, starting straight after breakfast, and trying to fit in a good seven hours so he could run or work out later in the day, and relax in the evening before bed. Ewan was working at home today too, so when Ryan paused to refuel on caffeine he went up the second flight of stairs to the top floor and knocked on Ewan's door.

"Come in."

Ryan stuck his head around, "Hey, man. I'm making coffee. Do you want some?"

"Oh fuck yes please. I'd love some. But don't bother to bring it up. I need to eat too, so I'll be down in a few."

"Okay."

Ewan joined Ryan in the kitchen just as he was pouring the coffee. He'd made it strong, which was how he liked it, so he added a little extra water for Ewan and put sugar in both.

"Yours is in the red mug."

"Cheers." Ewan put a couple of slices of bread in the toaster.

Seeing food made Ryan realise he was peckish. He'd had breakfast early, and it wasn't far off midday now. Opening his cupboard, he got out some muesli. Breakfast cereal was a lifesaver when you were hungry but lazy.

Once he'd filled a bowl and added milk, he leaned against the kitchen counter to eat it rather than going to sit in the living room. He'd heard the TV on in there and didn't want to get sucked in to watching anything.

"So, what's going on with you and Johnny then?" Ewan asked.

Ryan paused, a spoon of cereal halfway to his mouth. He should have expected this. It was the first time he'd been alone with Ewan since Sunday when he'd seen him at Johnny's place. "Nothing much." He took the mouthful, giving himself a bit of thinking time as Ewan eyed him sceptically.

"Did you fuck him again?"

"Are you always this nosey?"

"You know I am." Ewan grinned. "I get it. It's none of my business. But I'm taking your response as a yes."

Ryan huffed in frustration. He couldn't win. "Okay, yes I'm fucking him."

"Oh, so it's a regular thing?"

"Yes. For now. It's not a relationship, just sex."

"Fuck buddies?"

"Yeah."

"Well good for you. It's nice to have something regular if it's fun. And I'm glad you've worked out your sexual identity crisis."

"Mmm," Ryan said noncommittally around a mouthful of cereal. Because he'd been doing a very good job of not thinking about that aspect of what he was doing with Johnny. He knew it was something he needed to deal with eventually. He couldn't deny that he wasn't as straight as he'd liked to believe for a long time. Maybe he was only attracted to quite femme men, but they were still men. Ryan couldn't hide from the fact that he was bisexual. What he needed to untangle was why he felt uncomfortable about that, and whether he wanted to be more open about it with other people in his life—like his other housemates, or even his family.

Ugh.

He had enough on his plate for now. That could wait. Well... as long as he could trust Ewan to keep his mouth shut. "Look, mate." He met Ewan's gaze, voice serious, "I'm honestly still not quite sure where I am with it all at the moment. This is very new for me, and my head's still a bit of a mess about it. So can you do me a favour and keep this to yourself for now? I'd rather the rest of our housemates didn't know about it. Because it's not serious, it probably won't last long, and I don't want everyone knowing my business."

Ewan studied him, a small frown furrowing his brow. "Yeah. It's okay, man. I get it."

"Thanks," Ryan said gratefully. His bowl was empty now so he put it in the dishwasher along with his spoon. "Right. I'm going to get back to work. See you later." He picked up his coffee.

"Yeah, happy studying."

JOHNNY TEXTED Ryan just after five:

Do you have a lab coat at home?

Ryan chuckled, and replied: *No, why?*

I want to play doctors. Can you get one?

Not today. But I could next time I go into my department. Maybe later this week.

Shame. Still on for tonight anyway?

Definitely, Ryan sent, and then added: *Yours at eight?*

Yep. See you then :) x

The kiss was new. Ryan paused for a moment, wondering if it meant anything. Then he decided that having sex with each other was more intimate than a kiss in a text message, so it probably wasn't a big deal and he should stop overthinking.

Okay x, he replied.

BY THE TIME Ryan rang Johnny's doorbell, he was knackered. He'd spent almost the whole day studying, partly because he needed to, and partly because when he was busy cramming his head full of facts he didn't have any mental energy left over to stress about Johnny and what it all meant. His brain was fried and although he'd been stuck at a desk or sitting on his bed with his notes most of the day, his body felt exhausted too, stiff and achy from lack of movement. Tomorrow, he needed to make the effort to get out for a run or hit the gym as a break from work, but tonight he'd have to rely on Johnny to give him a workout.

"Hi." Johnny gave him a smile as he let him in.

Ryan was relieved when it was Johnny who answered the door. He didn't care too much about Johnny's housemates seeing him, because apart from Ewan they didn't have much connection with Ryan's friends, but it was still less awkward this way. "Hey."

Johnny led him straight upstairs without even offering him a drink this time. Ryan was relieved, it felt better for him when this was clearly all about sex—not that Johnny had given any indication that he wanted anything more either.

There was already music playing in Johnny's room, and as soon as they were inside Johnny started to take off his clothes. Ryan stripped too, feeling faintly disappointed that they weren't starting with kissing. He preferred more of a build up to getting naked, but he could roll with this too. And when Johnny pushed Ryan down on his back on the bed and started blowing him, Ryan definitely wasn't complaining.

His cock was still mostly soft when Johnny started, but he hardened quickly with Johnny's practised mouth and tongue. Ryan wondered how many guys Johnny had done this for, and quickly clamped down on an unwelcome flash of jealousy. He had no right to feel like that.

Focusing on how it felt instead, he slipped his fingers through Johnny's silky hair and hummed in approval as Johnny took him deep. Johnny was stroking Ryan's thighs, hands gradually edging higher, and Ryan gasped when he started stroking and squeezing Ryan's balls.

Johnny pulled off and started to lick Ryan's balls instead. His mouth was warm and wet, and his tongue was a delicious tickle as he lapped. "Oh yeah, that's good." He spread his legs a little wider to give Johnny better access, and then tensed as Johnny licked lower still, sucking on the sensitive skin between his balls and arse. He moaned, because it felt good, but his heart was beating out of his chest and not just because he was horny. Johnny put his hands on the backs of Ryan's thighs and pushed, lifting

Ryan's feet off the bed and tilting his arse up as he slid his mouth down, down, down....

Ryan drew in a shocked breath as Johnny licked into his crack, just grazing Ryan's hole with his tongue on each pass. Every muscle in Ryan's body was tight, poised on a knife-edge of indecision. To put a stop to this or let it happen? It felt good physically, but mental alarm bells were ringing all over the place. He hadn't expected Johnny to go there without at least asking first and Ryan was worried about what he might do next if Ryan didn't call a halt.

Johnny must have sensed Ryan's reluctance, because he stopped after a few licks and let Ryan's feet back down onto the bed, making Ryan feel grounded and immediately less vulnerable. "You not into that then?" Johnny asked. "Sorry, I should have checked. I forgot who I was with for a minute."

That was a sharp reminder that he was just one of many notches on Johnny's metaphorical bed post. "Yeah. Not really I don't think."

"You ever tried it?"

"No. But I never liked the idea of someone playing with my arse."

"Didn't it feel good though?"

"It was good, but it feels a bit...."

"Too gay?" Johnny raised his eyebrows.

Ryan didn't answer, because Johnny had hit the nail on the head.

Johnny rolled his eyes. "Don't worry. I get it. But it's your loss. You're missing out if you never find your prostate." He took Ryan's cock in his hand. "I'm sorry, I killed your boner. Want me to blow you again?"

"Yeah." Blowjobs were safe, especially when Ryan was on the receiving end.

It took him a little while to get back into it, but Johnny was skilled enough that he had Ryan ready to come within a few minutes. "I'm pretty close," he warned, hoping that Johnny would want to be fucked. But Johnny just paused to say, "Okay. Come in my mouth," before getting back to work. Ryan looked down. Johnny's face was mostly obscured by his hair, and one arm was down between his legs, moving rhythmically as he jerked himself off while he sucked. Letting his head fall back on the bed again, Ryan closed his eyes and enjoyed the building wave of approaching climax until it crashed over him and he groaned as his body tensed with the force of it.

Johnny sucked him more gently for a moment, then finally released him. He crawled up the bed and leaned over Ryan. "How do you feel about kissing someone after they've swallowed your come?"

Ryan answered him by putting a hand on the back of his neck and guiding him down. Johnny's hair fell around them like a curtain as they kissed. Ryan could taste himself faintly on Johnny's tongue. The bump of Johnny's erection against his hip reminded him that he ought to reciprocate.

"Do you want me to blow you?" he asked.

"Not today." Johnny reached for the lube from the bedside table and handed it to Ryan, then lay on his back beside him. "Finger me while I jerk off."

Ryan knelt between Johnny's thighs and slid two wet fingers into his crack while Johnny stroked himself. Johnny spread his legs wider. "Yeah. Put them in me."

One finger went in easily, so Ryan added the second and felt more resistance. He eased them in slowly, and Johnny moaned. "Oh yeah, that's good." Encouraged, Ryan started to thrust them in and out. "No. Go slowly. Yeah... that's better."

Ryan watched Johnny's expression relax into one of bliss as he slowed his movements to a sensual slide. "That good?"

"Mmm," Johnny hummed contentedly, his hand moving slowly over his cock. "So good." He began to stroke a little faster. "Twist your hand so your fingers are pointing up." More stroking, and his breathing was getting faster too. "Now curl them up a little. Oh fuck, yes. There. Keep going." Johnny's hand slowed again. He swiped at the precome on the tip of his cock and smeared it down the shaft, making it shine. Then he gripped his cock tightly, body taut and straining, hips canted up. Ryan hesitated. "Don't stop!" Johnny said urgently. "Go faster now."

Ryan pumped his fingers in and out, trying to get that same angle that Johnny had approved of. It seemed to be working because Johnny said, "Oh yeah. That's amazing. You're going to make me come." Johnny still wasn't stroking his dick, but he squeezed around Ryan's fingers and groaned loudly as white come erupted from the tip, splashing onto his stomach. Ryan kept going, pushing through the resistance as Johnny's muscles clenched around him and Johnny cried out as a second spurt hit his chest, and a third, and then a fourth. Head back and eyes screwed shut he seemed lost in his own ecstasy. "Fuck yes," he said weakly. "Slow down a bit." A few more gentle slides of Ryan's fingers elicited a final weak dribble and only then did Johnny move his hand again, catching the last bit of come and stroking himself with it as he clenched around Ryan's fingers one more time. "Stop now."

Ryan gently eased his fingers free and Johnny let his hips drop back onto the bed. He opened his eyes and raised his head to give Ryan a satisfied smile. "Fuck that was good."

"It looked it," Ryan admitted. "I never come for that long."

"And that's the magic of the prostate, which is why you should give it a try. If you don't want me to stick something up your arse, do yourself a favour and try it on yourself at home. Seriously. You won't regret it."

So that was why Johnny had wanted Ryan to finger him. Sneaky fucker. Ryan had to admit that this little display had him intrigued, but he didn't like being manipulated. He wanted time to think about it before he agreed to anything. "We'll see." He got up and started dressing.

"Want to meet again tomorrow night for some more stress relief?" Johnny asked.

Ryan hesitated. That would make three days in a row, which seemed a little un-casual. But he wanted Johnny, and this was a great way to wind down after revising. He was definitely sleeping better for it. "Okay."

"Is nine o'clock okay though? I'm working late tomorrow."

"Yes sure."

"And can you get that lab coat? Might be fun." Johnny was still lying naked on the bed covered in come. He grinned at Ryan suggestively. It was hard to resist him when he looked like that.

"Yeah, all right."

"Cool."

Ryan leaned down to kiss him on the cheek before leaving, and went home with a smile on his face.

TEN

Johnny checked his phone on his late afternoon coffee break, and found a message from Ryan sent an hour or so ago that nearly made him fall off his chair in surprise:

If I bring the lab coat, will you be the doctor?

He re-read it a couple of times; wanting to be sure he'd got it right before replying:

Sure, we can do that. What sort of examination will you require? He decided to be cautious. He didn't want to jump to the wrong conclusion and freak Ryan out again. The poor guy had gone as stiff as a board when Johnny had tried to lick his arse yesterday.

But Ryan's reply came back immediately as though he'd been waiting for Johnny to answer. And the message was gloriously unambiguous:

A prostate examination.

Johnny stared at the words, a flush prickling his skin as he imagined Ryan letting him do that. The idea of getting his fingers inside Ryan was insanely hot, and Johnny wasn't even entirely sure why he wanted it so much. He'd always been more of a bottom than a top. Topping was okay, but it wasn't Johnny's favourite. Bottoming took him to places that topping couldn't. Coming when he had a cock in his arse was infinitely more intense and amazing than the alternative, so right from the first time he tried it—okay the second time, because the first time he hadn't used enough lube and that hadn't been great—Johnny had always preferred to bottom, and was very happy hooking up with guys who were 100 percent tops. The more attention his own arse got the better as far as Johnny was concerned.

Yet the idea of introducing Ryan to his prostate was incredibly appealing. He wondered whether Ryan would ever want to try being fucked. Johnny hoped he might; it would be awesome to be the first to do that for him.

Shaking himself out of his daydreams, Johnny quickly typed: *I can definitely take care of that.*

Thank you, doctor.

Johnny grinned. Ryan was in role already? If that's how they were going to play it, Johnny could give as good as he got.

I'll see you in my office at 9 p.m. sharp then.

JOHNNY HAD a quick snack when he got home, then hurried to shower. Afterwards, he dressed in the most formal clothes he owned: a pair of grey trousers he'd bought for interviews and a shirt and tie. He reckoned that would help him look the part. Leaving his eyeliner off for once, he tied his hair back. Eyeing himself critically in the mirror he thought it was a shame he didn't wear glasses. Glasses would have perfected the sexy doctor look.

Next he tidied his desk, leaving out his laptop and a pad of paper and pen because he thought those added to the fantasy. Finally he laid out the lube, some tissues, and some latex gloves that he'd nicked from the first aid kit at work. Doctors probably used K-Y Jelly rather than Back Door Relaxing Anal Glide, but this would have to do.

It was only when he heard the doorbell that Johnny realised he probably shouldn't go down to answer the door dressed like this, otherwise his outfit would lead to all sorts of awkward questions. Ryan having to interact with one of Johnny's housemates was definitely the lesser of two evils. So Johnny cracked his door open and listened. Sure enough, Shawn yelled up the stairs, "Johnny, you've got a visitor."

"I'm in my room," Johnny called back. "Come on up." He quickly closed the door, then stationed himself in his desk chair, laptop open in front of him pretending to look busy while his heart pounded hard with nerves and anticipation. His browser was open at a page about rectal examinations, because that seemed appropriate.

There was a knock on his door.

"Come in," he said, keeping his eyes on the screen until he heard the door open. Then he turned, spinning around on his desk chair, and gave Ryan a polite smile and a nod.

Ryan stood uncertainly in the doorway, a carrier bag in one hand. "Here's the lab coat."

"Thanks." Johnny stood and held out his hand to take it as Ryan approached. He got it out and pulled it on quickly, brushing out the creases.

"Hello, Mr, um...." Johnny realised he didn't know Ryan's surname.

"Ellis," Ryan replied quickly.

"Have a seat, Mr Ellis."

Johnny gestured to the bed. It would have been good if he could have borrowed a chair from downstairs, but again, that would have led to questions.

"Thank you." Ryan sat down. His lips twitched as

though he was trying not to grin, and his cheeks were flushed pink. He was dressed casually in jeans, a T-shirt, and a hoodie with his usual trainers.

"So, what can I do for you today?"

"I'm here for a prostate examination," Ryan said, flush deepening.

"Okay, Mr Ellis. And is there any reason for that?" Johnny asked. "Have you had any problems?"

"Uh, no. Not really." Ryan shrugged. "I just thought it would be a good idea to have it checked."

"Yes that's very wise. I recommend that all men check their prostates regularly. If I do that for you today, then I can show you how to find it yourself in future. Sometimes massaging it can be very beneficial. It's good for releasing tension." Johnny couldn't help giving Ryan a dirty grin.

Ryan's mask slipped as he smiled too, then he cleared his throat and composed himself again. "Yes. So I've heard. So perhaps you can give me some tips on how to do that."

"Absolutely. Okay." Johnny rubbed his hands together briskly. He picked up the latex gloves and started to pull them on. Ryan's eyes widened. "Just drop your trousers and underwear and bend over for me. You can lean on the desk, or get on all fours on the bed if you prefer." Johnny gave Ryan the choice, so that he'd feel a little more in control and hopefully more comfortable.

Ryan chose the desk. Johnny turned away to give him some privacy, making sure the gloves were in place as he listened to the rustle of clothing and movement behind him. "Are you ready?"

"Yes," Ryan said.

Johnny picked up the lube and turned back. *Fuck.* The sight of Ryan bent over his desk sent a jolt of heat to Johnny's groin. He was reminded vividly of Ryan fucking him in this position, and the role reversal here was a huge turn on.

Ryan's head was hanging down and he didn't look at Johnny as he approached. His fists were clenched where they rested on the desk, betraying his tension.

"Right, Mr Ellis. This won't hurt, but it may be a little uncomfortable at first, and the lubricant will feel cold. I need you to try and relax for me." Johnny kept his voice smooth and professional, which was a challenge when he had a boner tenting his slacks. A quick glance down showed that Ryan's dick was soft, and Johnny wished he could suck Ryan first to get him in the mood, but Ryan seemed very much in his role as patient and Johnny didn't want to spoil that. "If you need me to stop at any point, just say. Okay?" Johnny said meaningfully, hoping Ryan understood that was Johnny talking and not the doctor.

"Okay." Ryan met his gaze for a second and Johnny saw a flash of comprehension that reassured him.

Heart pounding and hands shaking a little, Johnny slicked the forefinger of his right hand. Then he squeezed out an extra blob of lube onto the tip. "Spread your legs a little, please." Ryan obeyed, widening his stance. But his hole was still buried between the firm muscles of his glutes. Johnny used his left hand to part Ryan's cheeks, and there it was. Small and tight, and looking remarkably unwilling to be penetrated.

Ryan tensed as Johnny rubbed the blob of lube in, making the muscle even tighter at first. "Try and relax please, Mr Ellis. It will be more comfortable for you if you can."

"Sorry," Ryan said shakily.

Johnny kept rubbing gently in small circles. "Take a deep breath, and then let it out slowly. Try and relax on the exhale." Ryan sucked in a breath and blew out. Johnny felt a slight give. "That's good, and again." On the second exhale there was more noticeable unclenching. Johnny just kept rubbing, taking his time, exerting gentle pressure. Finally after a few more breaths the tip of his finger slipped in. Jesus, he was tight. Ryan tensed again, but only for a couple of seconds before consciously relaxing and letting Johnny push in a little deeper.

"Is that all right?" Johnny asked.

"Feels weird." Ryan's voice sounded as tense as his arsehole was.

"It will do if this is a new experience. Just let your body get used to it as long as it's not too painful."

"It doesn't hurt, it's just... really strange."

Johnny pushed in further. With him standing it was hard for him to get the angle to reach for Ryan's prostate, but for now he was just focused on getting Ryan comfortable with having something inside him. He slid his finger in and out slowly, feeling Ryan gradually relax and open a little more. Once Johnny thought Ryan was ready, he said, "I'm going to get a little more lube." He carefully let his finger slip free and picked up the bottle of lube again. Then he sat down in his desk chair and positioned himself slightly to the side where he could lean forward to see Ryan's cock. He was still soft, but Johnny wasn't discouraged. This was a new experience for Ryan, and some guys didn't get very hard with stuff in their butt even when they were really into it. As long as Ryan was happy to carry on, then he'd stick with it. "It will be easier for me to reach your prostate from here. Is it okay if I try again?"

"Yes."

The fact that his finger went back in easily was a positive sign. Now he was seated it was easy for Johnny to curve his finger forward. He pumped it gently in and out a few times until Ryan gasped.

Pausing, Johnny asked, "Is that a good sound or a bad sound?"

"Not sure," Ryan managed. He looked down between his legs to where his cock was starting to thicken and lift. "I guess it's good? But it kind of feels like I'm going to piss myself."

"That's normal," Johnny said. "You won't though, don't worry. Are you okay for me to continue with the examination?"

"Yes, doctor." Ryan glanced sideways and gave Johnny a quick grin before letting his head hang down again.

Johnny went back to sliding his finger in and out, trying to focus on the spot that had made Ryan gasp before. "Everything feels normal, you'll be glad to know. And please don't be embarrassed about getting an erection, that's a very usual reaction. I'm sure you know that the prostate is an erogenous zone. I'm used to this happening with my patients. Some men even ejaculate from having their prostates stimulated."

"So I believe." Ryan sounded a little breathless. His cock was more than half-hard now, Johnny watched it slowly crank up a little higher as he carried on with what he was doing.

"Well your prostate is definitely normal. Would you like me to carry on massaging it for you while you're here? As I said before, prostate massage can be very beneficial. Also, research shows that regular ejaculation reduces your risk of prostate cancer."

"Is that actually true?" Ryan turned to meet Johnny's gaze, and Johnny knew that question was all Ryan and not part of the role play.

"Yeah it is." Johnny grinned. Then he put on his serious face again. "Of course, Mr Ellis. You can trust me on that. I am a doctor after all."

Ryan chuckled. "Yes of course."

"How about we try something different, so I can get a little deeper. If you take off your shoes and the lower half of your clothes then you can kneel on the bed. That way it will be even easier for me, and I can try using two fingers if you think you're ready for more."

"Um. Okay."

Johnny stopped again, pulling his finger out so Ryan could straighten up and get out of his clothes. He took his hoodie off too, but left the T-shirt on. Johnny approved of that, having him partly clothed helped the fantasy. And Johnny was really enjoying the fantasy. He'd thought he would have enjoyed being on the receiving end more, and while he was sure he'd like that too, he was loving being the sexy doctor in charge of the situation. It helped that it was clearly doing it for Ryan.

Ryan crawled onto the bed but he went a little too far. Johnny wanted to stay standing, it helped him stay in role. "That's great, Mr Ellis, but can you shuffle back this way a little so I can reach you? And then spread your thighs a little wider. That's better." With Ryan kneeling on the edge of the bed Johnny had perfect access to his arse. He'd also be able to touch his cock, which was hanging down, thick, hard, and tempting. Johnny's mouth watered at the thought of sucking it, but that definitely wouldn't be very professional. To be fair, a doctor wouldn't offer to massage someone's prostate either but there were limits to how far you could suspend your disbelief in a role play situation.

Johnny slicked his fingers again. "Right, let's get back to this then. Are you ready?"

"Yes."

Johnny pushed the first one back into Ryan who gave a little huff as it slid home. After working that in and out a few times, Johnny withdrew it almost all the way and introduced a second fingertip. He pushed in slowly, it felt really tight with two and Ryan groaned as he worked him inside.

"Okay?" Johnny asked.

"Yeah," Ryan bit out.

"You sure?" Johnny moved them experimentally, curving them, and rubbing the front wall where he knew it should feel good.

"It's good. Just... intense." Ryan was breathless, but his cock was still hard and as Johnny kept up the slow slide of his fingers precome beaded at the tip.

"Is it okay if I touch your c— um... penis?" Johnny winced. Penis wasn't a sexy word, but it seemed more fitting. "That should help with the release we're trying to achieve."

"Yeah," Ryan said again. He was rocking back gently with each thrust of Johnny's fingers now, and Johnny wondered if he was aware he was doing it. It was hot as fuck.

Wrapping his hand around Ryan's cock, Johnny wished he wasn't wearing a glove on that one too, but he wasn't going to stop to take it off now and ruin the moment. The latex was thin enough that he could feel the heat of Ryan's skin through it. Lube would have been good too, but the slide of Ryan's foreskin should be enough. He gripped the shaft tight and started to stroke in time with the movement of his fingers.

Ryan moaned and his muscles squeezed tight. "God, that feels amazing."

Johnny carried on, going a little faster. "That's good, Mr

Ellis. Remember what I'm doing so you can try this for yourself at home if you need to." He was a little breathless himself now. "I recommend you purchase a suitable tool to help you. There are various places online where you can buy something that will work."

"Yeah. Fuck. I might have to. Holy *shit* that's good." He gasped out a chuckle. "Excuse my language, Doctor."

"You're excused. That's it, Mr Ellis. Just let go. Get out of your head and let your body do its thing." That was why Johnny loved being fucked so much. Having something in his arse took him places he rarely got to without that type of stimulation. He'd literally lose himself in the physical sensation of it, with no headspace left for feeling self-conscious. He wanted Ryan to experience that.

Groaning and wordless now, Ryan was rocking back on Johnny's fingers in a way that suggested he was getting there. Johnny kept quiet, not wanting to distract him again and pull him out of his body and into his head. He carried on with the insistent thrust of his fingers while he gripped Ryan's cock a little tighter and stroked faster.

"Yes. Like that," Ryan managed. "I'm gonna come...."

Johnny was glad about that because his arm was starting to ache. It had been an error of judgement to use his dominant hand in Ryan's arse instead of on his dick. He pushed through the pain, focusing on Ryan as Ryan muttered, "Yes, fuck... *yes*...." Finally the first spurt of come rewarded Johnny for his efforts and Ryan's voice rose, gasping out, "Ohmygod," before he gave another loud wordless cry and shot again, harder, his cock jerking as he shot thick, creamy come all over Johnny's bed while his arse squeezed Johnny's fingers. Johnny slowed his movements, then stilled when he thought Ryan was done.

"Fuck," Ryan said weakly. Then he looked at Johnny

over his shoulder. "That was amazing. But was I really loud?"

"Yeah a bit." Johnny grinned. "We forgot music today."

"You wouldn't have music in a doctor's office."

"True." Johnny let go of Ryan's cock and let his fingers slowly slide out.

"My legs are shaking." Ryan flopped onto his side and shuffled back to lie sprawled out, softening cock wet on his belly. "I think you broke me."

"In a good way?" Johnny got a couple of tissues and started to mop up Ryan's mess.

"In a brilliant way."

Ryan closed his eyes. He looked totally spent; relaxed and shattered. Johnny knew that feeling so well and he envied it, but he was happy that Ryan was getting to experience it. Looking at him, Johnny felt a spike of tenderness, an unexpected green shoot pushing through winter soil. He slipped the lab coat off and hung it on the back of the chair, then stripped down to his underwear. Climbing onto the bed beside Ryan, he put an arm across his chest and kissed his cheek. "You okay?" he murmured quietly.

"Yeah." Ryan turned his head to kiss Johnny's lips, a soft, sleepy press. His T-shirt was damp with sweat. Johnny pushed his hand beneath it to stroke his chest, which was clammy where sweat was cooling. As Johnny stroked him lightly, gooseflesh rose in the wake of his fingers.

It didn't look like Ryan was ready to move. "Want to get under the covers for a minute?" Johnny asked.

"Mmm."

"Shift your arse then."

Ryan huffed with the effort, but they managed to get under the duvet rather than on top of it. Johnny put an arm around Ryan and Ryan rested his head on Johnny's shoulder. "You never got off. Want me to jerk you off or anything?"

"Nah. I'm good." Johnny's arousal had passed now, but he was sure the memory of their role play would fuel a spectacular wank later. Ryan's loss of control had been amazing to facilitate. He reached across with his free arm to stroke Ryan's hair, combing his fingers slowly through the strands.

"Feels good," Ryan mumbled, so Johnny carried on.

Gradually, Ryan's breathing slowed, and the weight of his head on Johnny's shoulder got heavier. As Ryan drifted into sleep, Johnny's thoughts whirled, tangled and troubled. He couldn't deny he was starting to feel something for Ryan, something beyond the physical. Perhaps it was the regularity, seeing Ryan three days in a row was a lot. Johnny's usual arrangements were much more occasional. The growing intimacy between them made him nervous because it wasn't what either of them were looking for. Johnny didn't want to start expecting things. Life had taught him that expectations were dangerous. He should probably slow things down a little, put some space between them. It seemed like the sensible thing to do, so why did he feel so reluctant to do it?

He sighed, hating how much he liked the warm weight of Ryan in his arms and the comfort of him in his bed. It was tempting to let him sleep, to see how Ryan reacted when he woke naturally and realised where he was.

But no.

Johnny needed to set some boundaries and they had to start here. He shifted his hand to Ryan's cheek and patted gently. "Hey, man. You need to wake up and get back to your own bed."

"Mmph." Ryan jerked upright and rubbed his eyes. "Yeah, sorry."

"No worries. A good orgasm will do that to a guy." Johnny kept his voice light. He got up and pulled on a T-shirt and sweatpants, needing some clothes as armour to cover his sudden uncomfortable vulnerability.

He heard the creak of the bed, and the shuffle of movement and rustle of clothes. Johnny resisted the urge to watch as Ryan dressed.

"Okay. I'll leave you in peace. Thanks for tonight, it was... interesting."

Interesting was one word for it. Johnny finally turned to meet Ryan's gaze. His expression was uncertain, a little wary. Johnny wished he could see into his head and know what he was thinking. Maybe he was freaking out as much as Johnny was. All the intimacy of a few minutes ago had vanished like smoke on the breeze.

"Want to get together again soon?" Johnny asked before he could think better of it. Then he quickly added, "Maybe over the weekend?"

There was a moment of silence where Johnny could feel his pulse thumping.

Ryan shrugged. "Yeah, probably. I'm not sure what I'm up to. I'll text you." He sounded distant and he fiddled with the zip on his hoodie so he didn't have to meet Johnny's eyes. Was he already regretting what they'd done?

"Okay." Johnny felt as though a wall was going up between them, each of them adding a brick at a time. Maybe it was for the best. This was only ever supposed to be about sex. Ryan didn't want a boyfriend, and nor did Johnny. "Night then. Sleep well." Johnny kept his tone firm, a clear dismissal.

"Okay. Bye."

It was only after the door closed behind Ryan that

Johnny realised they hadn't kissed each other goodbye like they always had before, and that made him feel shitty.

"Ugh." He flopped down on his bed, phone in hand, and before he could think too much about what he was doing, he opened Grindr for the first time since he'd started seeing Ryan. They'd made it clear this wasn't an exclusive thing, but this week it had started to feel like one. Perhaps that was what was making Johnny anxious and vulnerable. He didn't like depending on one person. He needed a distraction, and Grindr was the best place to find it.

ELEVEN

Ryan didn't sleep well.

Despite his physical exhaustion after the incredible orgasm he'd had from Johnny, sleep took a long time to come.

Unsettled yet weirdly exhilarated, he went over and over what had happened. At first he focused on the physical aspect of it, trying to come to terms with how unexpectedly enjoyable it had been to let someone do those things to him. That led to him wondering how it would feel to have Johnny's cock inside him, and then he got horny imagining it.

But later, doubts and anxiety crept in. Things had been a little cool between them when they parted. Ryan flushed when he remembered falling asleep on Johnny. How embarrassing. That was crossing a line; no wonder things had been awkward after. Fuck buddies was one thing but sleeping together was quite another. He'd deliberately blown off Johnny's attempts to make a plan for when to meet next, and now he regretted it. It was probably for the best if they cooled things off a little; this week had been intense. But Ryan couldn't help craving more of Johnny.

HIS ALARM DRAGGED him out of a deep sleep at half past ten the next morning. Groggy and irritable, it took two cups of strong coffee to get him in the frame of mind for revision, and even then he found himself thinking about Johnny way more than he was comfortable with.

He sighed, glaring at the notes on his desk. Johnny was a distraction he couldn't afford at the moment when his future was on the line. Perhaps Ryan should cut his losses and end things before they got more complicated? He'd got what he wanted; he'd explored his bi-curiosity and couldn't deny what he'd discovered. Johnny had served his purpose and Ryan should get out before he got attached and made a fool of himself. Johnny had been very clear that he wasn't interested in a relationship even if Ryan was—which he wasn't. Much as he liked Johnny, and the sex was great, he wasn't ready to deal with everything that a relationship with another guy would entail. Admitting his bisexuality to himself was one thing, but sharing it with the world was quite another.

Yet the thought of finishing things with Johnny made Ryan's stomach feel as if it had rocks in it.

With sheer Herculean effort he pushed his troubled thoughts aside and forced himself to focus on work for a while with some success. He studied all afternoon until his head felt as if it was overflowing with facts, and only then did he let his mind turn back to Johnny. His body thrilled at the memory of Johnny's touch and he flushed with mingled shame and desire at the sounds he'd made. How he'd begged for more—with his body if not with actual words—and Johnny had given him exactly what he'd needed.

Ryan's fingers touched his phone before he consciously

thought about what he was doing. He'd said that he'd text, though. And after seeing each other so much this week it didn't seem unreasonable to get in touch today. Maybe Ryan had misread Johnny's mood last night, and Johnny was waiting to hear from him.

Hey, how are you? He sent the message quickly before he could change his mind.

Johnny didn't reply immediately, so Ryan put his phone aside and tried to carry on working but his concentration was shot now. He stretched, back cracking as he did so after hours of hunching over his notes and laptop. His phone sat blank and silent in front of him.

Deciding he desperately needed some exercise, which he'd neglected this week, he got up and looked out of the window. It was early evening and still light outside. Patches of blue sky showed through grey and white clouds. Opening the window, Ryan felt an April chill in the air, so he put a long sleeved compression top under a running shirt. He was scrolling on his phone for a playlist to get him in the running mood, when it buzzed in his hand and a message from Johnny flashed up:

Not bad thanks. You?

Ryan's spirits lifted as he typed: *Okay, bored of working. Going for a run.* He hesitated a moment before adding: *Wanna meet up later?*

Johnny's reply came back quickly: *Sorry. Got plans already actually.*

The answer was a sharp jab, deflating the balloon of happiness as fast as it had filled. Particularly because Johnny hadn't suggested an alternative day to meet.

No worries, Ryan sent back. Then put his headphones in his ears, put his music on, and turned off notifications ready to run. Even if Johnny replied again he wanted some headspace for a while.

He wished he could turn off his thoughts as easily.

What's Johnny doing? Where's he going? Who's he seeing?

The questions echoed in Ryan's head in time with the beat of his trainers on the pavement as he ran. He muttered a curse. It was none of his business. He had no right to know how Johnny spent his time when they weren't together. Johnny was a free agent and could do whatever the hell he liked in his spare time—as could Ryan.

DISTRACTION THAT EVENING came in the form of James barging into Ryan's room after dinner. Ryan was still half-heartedly trying to revise, with limited success.

"I'm so done with studying today. I can't take any more," James said dramatically. "Please come to the pub with me? I need to get out somewhere other than the library for my sanity."

"Yeah, okay." Ryan needed something to stop him thinking about Johnny and what he might be doing, and who he might be doing it with. Alcohol and company should help with that.

"Cool. You're my saviour. I asked Colin too but he doesn't want to go, and Justine and Nadia went to the cinema."

"Ewan?" Ryan asked.

"Round at Dev's for dinner. Just for a change." James rolled his eyes, but in gentle amusement. They all knew Ewan was totally smitten and they'd given up trying to tease him about it. "Are you ready to go out soon?"

"Yeah. Give me five minutes to get out of sweatpants and into some jeans."

They ended up at the Old Duke, unsurprisingly as it was the nearest decent pub. Of course, being there reminded Ryan of Johnny. His eyes strayed to the fruit ciders lined up in the fridge behind the bar and the heavy weight was back in his stomach again at the thought of what Johnny's "plans" for tonight night involve.

It was busy tonight and there was a girl working behind the bar Ryan hadn't seen in there before. He caught her eye and she gave him a quick nod and a smile, and came to serve them when she was done with her previous customer. Ryan ordered a pint of beer for himself. "And what do you want, man?" he asked James.

"A pint of lager. I'll have the Stella please."

Ryan paid for both drinks with a tenner. "Thanks," he said as the girl placed the change in his hand.

She smiled. "You're welcome." She held his gaze just long enough to make Ryan wonder if she was showing more than a friendly interest.

As they carried their pints to a table, James nudged him. "I reckon you're in there, mate. You should give her your number or ask her out, assuming you're still into girls." They took their seats. "How did it go with Johnny on Sunday anyway? I never got a chance to ask you."

"It was okay."

"Did you hook up with him again?" James sounded interested, not in a challenging way, but Ryan hesitated, cheeks heating. He didn't want to lie, but didn't want to discuss what was going on with Johnny. The pause and his flush must have given him away. "I'll take that as a yes then. Seeing him again?"

Ryan flashed a guilty glance at James who grinned.

"Yeah. We're... fuck buddies. Nothing serious." Hoping that was enough to satisfy James's curiosity, Ryan turned the subject back to the girl at the bar. "So, you really reckon she fancies me?" Ryan looked back at the bar and caught the blonde's eye again. She gave him another smile before turning back to her customer. "It's hard to tell. She might just be being friendly."

"She didn't smile at me like that. She's hot. You lucky bastard. Wish it was me she'd noticed," James said glumly. "And you've already got someone to fuck. Life is so unfair."

Ryan glanced over again. The girl was busy so he was able to study her without her noticing. She was attractive; tall and curvy with long fair hair that shone when the light caught it, and she had a lovely smile. As she looked up and spoke to the man she was serving, Ryan noticed the dark smoky liner that ringed her eyes and, just like that, Johnny was front and centre in his head again.

He picked up his pint and took a few generous glugs.

Fucking Johnny.

Maybe Ryan needed to remind himself that Johnny wasn't the only person who could make him feel good. Next time he bought a round, he'd see if she still looked interested —and interesting.

BY THE THIRD ROUND, when it was Ryan's turn to buy again, he was loosened up by the alcohol and feeling bold. He deliberately timed his approach hoping the girl would be free to serve him, and it worked out perfectly.

"Hi." He gave her his most winning smile.

"Same again?" Soft pink lips parted as she grinned back.

"Yes please. You've got a good memory considering how many customers you've served tonight."

She shrugged. "Goes with the territory."

"What's your name?"

"Kerry," she replied. "Yours?"

"Ryan."

"Nice to meet you, Ryan." She grinned.

"Likewise."

Ryan studied her as she pulled his pint, her eyes cast downward. Her lashes were thick and dark, probably not real but it was a good look on her. Her practised movements as she dealt with the pump were confident, and that was attractive to Ryan too. An image of Johnny flashed into his mind, dressed in black with his hair falling over one black-ringed eye.

He and Johnny weren't exclusive. So there was nothing to stop Ryan chatting her up.

"You been working here long?" he asked. "I haven't seen you here before."

"No, only started a couple of weeks ago. I needed something to take the edge off my overdraft." She started pouring James's lager.

"You're a student at the uni then?"

"Yeah." Ryan was about to ask her what year and what subject, but she was already putting the drinks in front of him. "That'll be seven-twenty please."

He dug in his pocket for cash and gave her a tenner. When she came back with his change, he decided to go for it. "Can I buy you a drink sometime maybe? In a pub that you don't work in?"

"Oh." She flushed. "Thanks, but I have a boyfriend." She lowered her voice a little and added, "If I didn't then I would be interested. Just so you know...."

"It's okay, don't worry." Ryan's face burned. It was

always awkward being rejected even if there was a good reason. "He's a lucky guy."

"Thank you." Her smile was back, with a hint of regret as she handed him his change.

"No luck?" James said as Ryan sat down again. He'd been watching their exchange.

"Nah, she's with someone."

"She still liked you though."

"Yeah," Ryan admitted, his ego boosted despite the outcome.

He felt faintly relieved too. Although she was cute, he wasn't sure how he'd have felt about starting something with her when it was a knee-jerk reaction to being insecure about Johnny. He was being ridiculous anyway. For all he knew, Johnny was out with a mate tonight. And even if he *was* hooking up, what did it matter to Ryan? It didn't affect what they did together. If Johnny was able to keep his other hook ups separate then Ryan could too. It was just a different mindset he wasn't used to, because with girlfriends, even casual ones, the expectation was usually that you focused on one person at a time. Ryan could handle it; he simply needed to stop obsessing about Johnny when he wasn't with him and focus on other things instead—like James who had started talking to him about football, and Ryan had no idea what he was saying.

"Sorry, what? I was miles away."

James rolled his eyes and started again.

THEY STAYED for a fourth pint to even out the rounds, and by the time they walked home Ryan was pleasantly inebriated and feeling mellow and relaxed. Everything seemed better after a few drinks. His forthcoming exams felt manageable, he was excited about graduating and starting work, and was happy that he didn't need to move away. James was staying in Plymouth next year too, and so was Ewan. Ryan was glad that some of his mates would be sticking around.

His thoughts drifted to Johnny again and he wondered how long their arrangement would last. Determined to make it work, Ryan thought that maybe after his exams were over he could make more effort to hook up with other people so that it would feel more even. If he couldn't find girls who wanted no-strings sex, then he could probably find other guys to fuck. That wasn't such a bad idea now he knew he was into that. There must be guys on hook up apps who'd be his type, pretty, feminine-looking guys who he'd like as much as Johnny.

It was a solid plan and Ryan was feeling much happier now he'd decided on it.

When they got back to the house James fumbled with his keys on the doorstep, trying and failing to get them into the lock.

"Hurry up," Ryan grumbled.

"I can't find the hole," James said, and then he snorted. "That's what she said. Or maybe he...."

Ryan chuckled. Then there was a jingle as James dropped his keys. "Oh for fuck's sake."

The front door of the neighbouring house opened, and a shaft of light spilled out as James scrabbled around. Ryan crouched down to help him.

"Thanks, sexy," a deep voice said. "I'll add you to my favourites in case you fancy a repeat."

Ryan looked up to see a man step out of the house next door. He looked a little older than Ryan, maybe in his thirties, with short cropped hair, and a dark beard.

Ryan's stomach lurched when he saw Johnny silhouetted in the doorway behind him. "Yeah, that was fun. Cheers," Johnny said.

The man left, his footsteps heavy down the path.

Caught like a rabbit in headlights, Ryan stared at Johnny, his heart pounding, not wanting to be seen but unable to look away.

"Got the fuckers!" James said triumphantly, standing with his keys in his hand.

Johnny visibly started, putting a hand on his chest as he wheeled around. "Fuck, you made me jump."

"Sorry," James said. "Dropped my keys. Too much beer."

Only then did Johnny's gaze meet Ryan's. Frozen, Ryan was still crouched on the ground like an idiot. He straightened up, legs wobbly from beer, and the adrenaline coursing through him. Until he'd seen it with his own eyes he hadn't really believed Johnny was busy fucking someone else tonight. Now with the evidence in front of him, his imagination crystallised into cold reality, forming a lump of ice in his gut.

Knowing in theory that their arrangement was a casual, non-exclusive one was very different to seeing it in practice. Ryan had tried to convince himself that his relationship with Johnny was purely friends with benefits, no feelings involved, but his reaction to seeing Johnny with someone else brought that illusion crashing down. Suddenly Ryan had an awful lot of feelings about what was happening, and none of them were good. When he thought about the intimacy of their encounters, he felt sick imagining Johnny sharing that with another guy—with lots of other guys. Ryan had tried to tell himself that what he'd been doing with Johnny was just about sex, but now with painful clarity he realised it wasn't, not for him anyway. It might be based on sexual attraction, but Ryan had made himself vulnerable mentally and emotionally as well as physically and that meant something to him.

Obviously it didn't mean so much to Johnny.

"Good night then?" Johnny said casually. But a muscle clenched in his jaw.

Ryan couldn't find the words to answer, but luckily James didn't seem to notice the tension. "Yeah, few beers down the Old Duke. Always a good way to end the week," he said cheerfully. "See you." He stumbled inside.

Ryan tore his gaze away from Johnny and followed James, ignoring Johnny's muttered, "Bye then."

"Wanna play *Call of Duty*?" James asked. "I might have another beer too. I've worked hard all week. I can afford a hangover tomorrow."

"Yeah." More beer and video games sounded like an excellent plan. Ryan didn't want to be alone with his thoughts at the moment.

Ryan lost track of time as they played. They had a couple more beers each, and it was only the gaming that stopped Ryan from drinking too fast. Johnny hovered at the edge of his consciousness but Ryan kept him at bay by ruthless focus on the game.

"Oh hey, guys." Ewan and Dev came in to join them. They snuggled up together on the other sofa, Ewan scrolling on his phone as they talked quietly together.

Next time they reached a pause in the game, James put his controller down and yawned. "I'm done. Too tired to play."

"Ah fuck, really? Anyone else want to join me?" Ryan asked, not ready to stop.

"No, I'm not in the mood for gaming. Can we put the

telly on instead?" Ewan looked up from his phone. "There's a film starting soon that we were hoping to watch."

"Ugh." Ryan huffed, frustrated. "I suppose so."

"You sure?" Dev asked. "We can always record it."

"No. It's fine. Sorry. I was still in the gaming zone. Didn't mean to sound pissy."

"Thanks." Ewan put his phone down on the coffee table and settled back on the sofa with his arm around Dev. Dev let his head drop on Ewan's shoulder. He looked like he was ready for a nap rather than a movie. Ewan took Dev's hand and linked their fingers together. Ryan watched as he squeezed Dev's hand gently, and he felt a corresponding squeeze around his heart. Witnessing their happiness was an extra slap in the face after a shitty evening. When he tore his gaze away he saw Ewan watching him curiously.

Standing up quickly he said, "I'm heading to bed. Night all." He left the room in a rush, going straight upstairs, and into the bathroom.

After he'd pissed and brushed his teeth Ryan let himself out to find Ewan waiting outside. "It's all yours." He stood aside, gesturing to the bathroom door.

"Are you okay?" Ewan asked.

"Why wouldn't I be?" Ryan scowled.

Ewan raised his eyebrows. "You tell me? Whatever, man. If you don't want to talk about it...." He raised his hands and pushed past Ryan into the bathroom.

Ryan went into his room and stripped down to boxers and a T-shirt before getting into bed. Turning off the lamp, he lay in the darkness. His head was spinning a little from the alcohol. He was too tired and too drunk to think clearly now, but at least the booze would probably help him sleep. In the morning he'd try and sort out his tangled thoughts.

TWELVE

Johnny lay awake.

Curled on his side, he stared at the faint orange halo around his window where the light from the streetlamps outside crept in around the edges of the curtains.

He hugged his pillow and tried to ignore the gnawing anxiety in his belly, willing sleep to come. His body was tired, physically sated from fucking Carl—the guy he'd hooked up with earlier—but his mind was unsettled and restless.

Even before the encounter with Ryan on the doorstep, Johnny had been feeling weird about things. He'd got talking to Carl last night. They'd swapped photos and discussed their preferences. They seemed compatible so Johnny had invited him around this evening for sex. Nothing new there.

Carl had been a good fuck and they'd both had fun, so why had Johnny been left feeling unsatisfied and uneasy?

Ryan seeing Carl leaving was unfortunate. But Johnny had established clear expectations with Ryan at the start of their arrangement, and one of those was that this wasn't an exclusive thing. They were both free to see other people if they wanted, so there was no need for Johnny to be feeling this nagging sense of guilt.

With a heavy sigh he rolled onto his back and let his thoughts keep spinning, hoping that maybe if he slept on it, everything would make more sense when he woke.

JOHNNY HAD a long and busy day at work on Saturday, with very little time to think about Ryan. He checked his phone every time he took a break, but there was nothing from Ryan. The guilt of last night had persisted and Johnny was frustrated with himself for feeling it. No matter how many times he told himself he hadn't done anything wrong, he felt shitty about what had happened. He kept picturing Ryan's face as he stared at Johnny after Carl had left. Shock and surprise, and poorly concealed hurt were written all over it.

He still hadn't heard anything from Ryan by the time he got home. He thought about texting but he wasn't sure what he should say. He didn't need to explain or apologise, but he couldn't help feeling the urge to contact Ryan and justify what he'd seen.

When Sid texted to ask him if he wanted to meet for a drink, Johnny accepted gratefully, glad of the distraction.

They met in a pub near Sid's flat, where they always used to drink when they'd lived there together.

"No Ben tonight?" Johnny asked as they stood at the bar waiting to be served.

"No, he's got an essay to finish. So you get me all to yourself."

"For once." Johnny grinned.

Sid and Ben were almost joined at the hip these days,

but it was hard for Johnny to mind when his best friend was so obviously happy.

Once they'd been served they sat down with their drinks and caught up on each other's news: jobs, families, and how they were getting on with their new living arrangements.

"It's quite different being in a big shared house after the flat with you," Johnny said. "But it's okay. Two bathrooms between six people is a pain in the arse sometimes, and the kitchen can be chaotic at busy times, but it's nice having more people around to hang with."

"And you're getting on okay with them all?" Sid asked.

"Yeah, they're good guys. I'm still surrounded by couples though—not much of a change in that regard." Johnny chuckled.

"You still having fun on Grindr? Got any new regulars?"

Johnny looked down at his cider for a moment so he didn't need to meet Sid's eyes. "No new regulars from Grindr, but I've been seeing a bit of Ryan. Remember him?"

Sid frowned for a moment before comprehension dawned. "Ryan from next door, who you got off with at Ben's birthday party?"

Johnny nodded. "Yeah."

"Wow, I thought that was just a one-off."

"It was. But then we started something last weekend and have met a few times since." Johnny picked at the label on his bottle, trying to sound casual.

"Nothing serious, I assume?" Sid knew Johnny well enough to know Johnny's aversion to relationships. He understood why too. Johnny's heart had been broken before they met at uni, but Johnny had eventually told him why he preferred to keep his distance emotionally. Sid had managed to slip through Johnny's defences once they'd decided early on that they were better as friends than lovers. Sid was the only guy that Johnny truly trusted not to hurt him.

"No, just the usual. Fuck buddies. That's how I like it."

"So you're both seeing other people?"

"Well, I am. I don't think he is. But he could if he wanted to."

That thought made Johnny imagine Ryan with other people. Ryan kissing a girl—or another guy—fucking someone else, letting them do the things he'd let Johnny do.

His stomach lurched.

What the hell? Johnny didn't do jealousy. Not anymore. He'd given it up at the same time he'd stopped allowing himself to get close to people. If you didn't trust people, or have expectations of them, then they couldn't hurt you and that was how Johnny liked it. He'd never cared about people he fucked hooking up with other people—as long as they used condoms and tested regularly. Why was the idea of Ryan with someone else making his cider taste sour? Then he remembered the expression on Ryan's face when he'd seen Johnny with Carl last night, and that made him feel even worse.

Something must have shown on Johnny's face because Sid was looking at him intently. "Is Ryan okay with you seeing other people?"

"I don't know. But he knows that's the deal." Ryan hadn't looked very okay about it last night.

"Agreements can change. Maybe you should talk to him if you're seeing each other regularly and find out how he feels."

"There's no way he wants a proper relationship," Johnny said dismissively. "He's only just realised he's bi and he's still mostly in the closet. He's experimenting while he works things out. He's not going to want to jump into something exclusive with me." Johnny wondered whether he was trying to convince Sid or himself.

Sid looked sceptical. "Has he told you all this?"

"Sort of. Some of it. Some of it I'm extrapolating."

"Maybe you should find out what he wants. It seems a bit unbalanced if you're the only one shagging other people."

"Yeah. Maybe." Johnny took a swig of his drink. Done with this conversation, he changed the subject. "So, how's cohabiting working out for you and Ben? Are you arguing about the washing up and whose turn it is to empty the bin yet?"

BACK AT HOME, Johnny turned over the conversation with Sid in his mind as he brushed his teeth and got ready for bed.

Sid's point about it being unbalanced had struck home, shining a light on something that had been bothering Johnny but that he hadn't been able to articulate. It made sense of his unexpected guilt over hooking up with Carl. Even if Ryan had agreed to them not being exclusive, that didn't mean he was happy about it. Johnny hadn't really given him much choice. He'd been the one to insist on no strings. Ryan had gone along with it, but that was last weekend and Johnny's feelings about Ryan had changed since then with the amount of time they'd spent together. Maybe Ryan's had too.

There was an intensity to their connection, an honesty and depth that didn't feel compatible with fucking other people unless they were both completely happy with having an open relationship. If Johnny was honest with himself, he wasn't happy with the idea of Ryan fucking around, so it was entirely possible that Ryan felt the same. But Johnny wasn't sure he was ready to talk to Ryan about changing the boundaries, because the idea of something more serious was terrifying.

Johnny let out a sigh of frustration as he got into bed. This was why he didn't like relationships. They were messy and complicated, and as soon as you let yourself start caring about another person there was the potential for being hurt —or for hurting someone else.

He turned off the light and curled onto his side. His bed felt big and empty, and it seemed like a long time since he'd seen Ryan even though it had only been a couple of days. His attachment to Ryan had crept up on him like a predator stalking unwary prey, and now Johnny was in its clutches it was too late to escape it. The gnawing ache in his chest scared him.

He didn't like feeling this vulnerable. It would probably be best to get out before he got any deeper, but he couldn't bring himself to finish things with Ryan.

ON SUNDAY MORNING, Johnny was still unsure about what to do. He and Ryan needed to talk, but Johnny wasn't sure what he wanted to say. Still mulling it over, he went downstairs to make coffee, only to find that some wanker had used the last of his milk and nobody else in the house had any either.

"Fuck's sake." He stamped upstairs to get dressed so he could nip out to the corner shop and buy some.

Once he was out, he realised it was a gorgeous day. At the end of the road, instead of turning right for the shop, he went left on an impulse and headed down through the town centre to pick up a takeaway coffee, then on towards Hoe Park. It was busy there today with dog walkers, joggers, kids on skateboards, old folk pottering, and parents out pushing prams and strollers. All the residents of Plymouth seemed to be out enjoying the spring sunshine and blue skies.

Johnny found an uninhabited bench and sat watching the world go by as he sipped his coffee, enjoying the warmth of the sun on his face. The sea glittered in the harbour, a deeper blue than the sky. One of the cross-channel ferries cut a swathe through the water, churning it up and leaving white wake behind.

Idly people-watching, Johnny's attention was caught by a lone runner. Tall and broad, there was something familiar about the set of his shoulders, and as he got closer Johnny realised who it was.

Ryan.

The route he was taking would pass right by Johnny's bench. Ryan had headphones in and was focused on the path in front of him, so Johnny stood and moved into Ryan's path, heart beating hard as their gazes locked and surprised recognition registered on Ryan's features. He stopped a few feet away, flushed, and panting. "Hey." He took his headphones out of his ears.

"Hi." Johnny tried to smile but his face felt stiff with nerves. "How are you?"

"Okay thanks. You?"

The awkwardness was painful as they stared at each other warily. Johnny was already regretting the impulse to catch Ryan's attention. This chance meeting hadn't given him time to plan what to say. He'd have to wing it. But at least it had saved him agonising over when to text, and what to type. "Not bad. You had a good weekend?"

Ryan shrugged. "Bit boring. Just revising yesterday, then I got up early to do more today. I needed a break, so here I am." He gestured around them.

Deciding to draw attention to the elephant in the room rather than continue to ignore it, Johnny said, "You were out on Friday night though. Did you have a good night?"

There was a silence and Ryan shifted his weight uneasily from foot to foot.

"Yeah. It was okay. I just had a few beers with James then went back and played some video games. How about you? Did you have fun with that bloke?"

"I guess. It wasn't the best.... Look, Ryan. I'm sorry if it was weird, seeing him and knowing...."

"Knowing you'd been fucking him." A muscle flickered in Ryan's jaw.

"Yeah. I was thinking maybe we should talk about—"

"There's nothing to say," Ryan said briskly. "We have an arrangement, I know you see other guys and that's fine. It's not like this is serious between us is it? It's just fucking."

Johnny searched Ryan's face for uncertainty, but the shutters were down. There was no hint of the softness or intimacy that Johnny had glimpsed last time they were alone together. Maybe Johnny had imagined it. Well, if Ryan didn't want anything more serious, then Johnny would keep his thoughts to himself. He'd try and deal with his feelings, and if that failed then he'd break it off with Ryan and move on.

"Right, okay then. As long as we're both on the same page."

"Yeah, yeah. Definitely. Look, I'd better finish my run. I'll get stiff if I stop for too long. I can meet later—if you want? Could do with letting off some steam this evening."

"Um, yeah," Johnny said, not sure whether to feel relieved or disconcerted. "What time?"

"Eight."

Relief won out. This was the best possible outcome. They could carry on as they were now Johnny knew exactly where he stood. "Okay. See you then."

THIRTEEN

Idiot, idiot, idiot, idiot....

Ryan's feet pounded with the rhythm of the voice in his head as he ran back home.

Running as fast as he could in the opposite direction from Johnny seemed like a sensible solution to his current dilemma. What had started as something fun and uncomplicated had rapidly become something very different. Yet like a hapless moth burning itself on a flame, Ryan couldn't stay away from Johnny even though he knew he was playing with fire.

Johnny had given him the perfect opportunity to be honest, and Ryan had bottled it. He should have told him that he wasn't comfortable with him seeing other people. The trouble was, that even after spending way too much time thinking about it yesterday, Ryan still didn't know what he really wanted from Johnny. Sure, he hated the thought of Johnny hooking up with other guys, but he couldn't very well ask Johnny to stop unless he was prepared to give him a good reason.

Hey, Johnny, I only want to be your fuck buddy, but I don't want you to fuck anyone else.

Ryan was pretty sure that wasn't the usual deal with fuck buddies, and it made him sound like a selfish twat who wanted to have his cake and eat it—or worse, someone who wanted to keep the cake all to himself, but only eat the icing and waste the rest of it. But what else could Ryan offer? He wasn't ready for an actual relationship with another guy. And even if he was, Johnny didn't seem to want that either. Ryan had two choices: cut his losses and stop fucking around with Johnny, or stick with it and deal with his jealousy.

It wasn't a hard choice to make. Option two meant he got to feed his Johnny addiction, so Ryan was going to give it a shot and try and make it work for now.

DETERMINED to keep his feelings under a tight rein, Ryan turned up at Johnny's a little after eight that evening. Johnny answered the door with a nervous smile. "Hi, want to come straight up?"

"Yeah."

"How was the rest of your day?" Johnny asked as he led the way upstairs.

"Not bad thanks. Spent most of it studying again."

Johnny opened the door to his room. "How long till your exams start now?"

"The week after next."

"Wow. Not long then."

"No." Ryan's gut clenched with nerves at the thought.

"Ready for some stress relief then?" Johnny raised his eyebrows, his grin more relaxed now.

"Yeah." Ryan moved closer, hoping that physical

contact would banish the last of the awkwardness between them. He reached for Johnny, pulling him into a kiss. Johnny kissed him back, and it felt good and right. The physical connection between them was easy and uncomplicated—chemistry, pure and simple. Ryan just needed to focus on that and enjoy it.

They started to undress each other, breaking the kiss as Ryan pulled Johnny's T-shirt over his head and then stripped off his own.

"What do you want to do tonight?" Johnny asked, already flushed and breathless as Ryan grabbed his hips and tugged him close again.

"I want to fuck you," Ryan said without hesitation. "Bend you over and stick my cock in your hole." He wanted to get back to what he was comfortable with, being in control. "But first I want you to suck my dick for me."

Johnny chuckled. "Sounds good." He reached between them and rubbed Ryan's erection through the sweatpants he was wearing. "I love sucking you, and I love it when you fuck me." He kissed Ryan again, slow and deep, before dropping to his knees on the floor and grinning up at him. "Easy access." He pulled Ryan's sweatpants and underwear down in one swift movement so his cock sprang free. He licked the tip, and teased Ryan with kisses, his expression mischievous as Ryan tried to push into his mouth but missed.

"Fucking take it," Ryan growled. He wrapped a hand around the base and put his other hand on the back of Johnny's neck, holding him where he wanted him as he pushed against Johnny's wet lips. "Like that." Johnny parted his lips and let Ryan thrust into his mouth. He looked up through his lashes, passive and obedient as Ryan fucked his mouth deeper. "Now suck it. Yeah. Perfect." Ryan tightened his fingers in Johnny's hair at the sensation of Johnny's throat tightening around him and the caress of his tongue.

Johnny hummed, his eyes closed as he focused on taking Ryan's dick and pleasuring Ryan at the same time. Ryan let him do it until he started to get close to coming. Then he pulled out and rubbed his wet cock over Johnny's lips, precome smearing and making them shine. Johnny smiled, trying to get Ryan's cock back in his mouth but Ryan wouldn't let him have it. "No. I need a break. Get up, and get naked." He toed off his trainers and got his sweatpants and underwear all the way off while Johnny stood and stripped for him.

"Where do you want me?" Johnny asked.

"On your hands and knees on the bed."

The bed creaked as Johnny got into position and Ryan moved in close behind him. Taking his cock in hand he guided it into Johnny's crack and thrust a few times, passing over his hole in a dry slide. Johnny gasped and pressed back against him. "Lube and condoms are in the drawer by the bed now. I moved them for easy access."

"Not ready for that yet." Ryan licked his fingers and rubbed those over the puckered skin instead; making it wet so his cock could slide better. He wished he could just stick his cock into Johnny. He'd love to know what it would feel like to fuck him bare, to fill him up with come. He groaned at the thought, grinding hard into Johnny's crack as more precome slicked the way.

Moving back, Ryan rubbed Johnny's hole with his fingers again. "Hold yourself open for me."

Johnny lay down, resting his head on the bed so he could reach back with both hands and part his arse cheeks. "Like that?"

"Oh fuck yes. You look so hot like that."

"Like a little slut waiting for your cock?" Johnny said breathlessly. "Or your tongue?"

"Yeah." Ryan's balls drew up at his words. "You want my tongue in your arse?"

"Yes. You're so good at that."

Ryan grinned, leaning forward to lick Johnny's hole. He teased him with light touches that made Johnny squirm and moan. "Oh yeah, that's amazing. More." Ryan kept going, and then added his fingers into the mix, first with spit, then pausing briefly to get the lube so he could go deeper.

"God, you look hot." He watched as he slid his fingers in and out slowly, trying to rub over where Johnny's prostate must be. He remembered how incredible it had felt when Johnny did this to him, and for a fleeting moment he wished he was on the receiving end.

"You gonna fuck me?" Johnny asked breathlessly.

"You want me to?"

"Yeah. Want your cock. Feels so good inside me."

Ryan pulled out his fingers and picked up the condom. "Fuck," he cursed, fingers slipping on the packet. "Open this for me."

Johnny tore it and passed the condom back.

"Thanks." Ryan rolled the rubber down his shaft and then added a little lube before lining himself up. He rubbed his cockhead over Johnny's hole not using quite enough pressure to breach him.

Johnny groaned in frustration. "Fucking tease! Hurry up." Chuckling, Ryan finally gave in and pushed deep inside making them both gasp as Johnny clenched around him with an "Oh-fuck-yesss!"

Ryan withdrew and thrust back in, probably more roughly than he should, but Johnny didn't ask him to slow down or stop. He was moaning and murmuring words of encouragement. Having Ryan's cock in him seemed to take him to new heights compared to Ryan's fingers. Ryan wondered how different it felt. He supposed it depended on the dick, but most guys' dicks were longer than their fingers. Johnny's definitely was, even though he wasn't as big as Ryan. Ryan found himself imagining how it might feel to have Johnny's cock inside him, fucking him like this.

The thought of it sent a flash of heat through him, and he fucked Johnny faster and harder. "God. Feels good," he muttered.

"Yeah." Johnny dropped forward onto an elbow, reaching one hand beneath him to stroke himself. "Oh yeah. It really does."

There was no conversation for a while, just the wet sounds of sex and ragged breathing with the occasional moan. Johnny jerked himself off slowly at first, but then he spread his legs a little wider making Ryan shift position slightly and suddenly he became frantic. "Oh fuck, yes. Don't stop." He moved his arm furiously. "Yeah, like that. You're going to make me come."

"Soon?" Ryan asked. Because he was right on the brink himself.

"Yeah."

Ryan bit his lip, the pain giving him a few extra precious seconds as he pounded into Johnny. The bed was creaking and for a fleeting moment Ryan remembered they were in a house full of people and hadn't put any music on to mask the sound. But then Johnny was moaning and clenching around his dick and they could have had a ticket-paying audience and Ryan wouldn't have cared. He moaned too, giving into the incredible wave of sensation as orgasm overtook him and he came, cock pulsing as he emptied his balls into Johnny, wishing there wasn't a condom between them.

They lay in a sweaty panting heap. Johnny flat on the bed with Ryan spread out on top of him. "Am I squashing you?" Ryan asked.

"Yeah, but I like it."

Ryan kissed Johnny's shoulder, then his cheek.

Johnny hummed and reached back to pat Ryan on the hip. "That was awesome."

"Mmm." Fucked out and contented, Ryan agreed. They were so good together.

As soon as his cock started to slip free, Ryan pulled out and dealt with the condom. Johnny moved when he did, and put his boxers and T-shirt back on so Ryan started to dress, not wanting to outstay his welcome this time and make things awkward again.

They stood, facing each other when Ryan was dressed. As soon as the sex was over, all the unspoken things in Ryan's head seemed to be occupying space between them. When they were fucking, nothing else mattered. Their sexual connection was easy and solid, but the rest was a mess as far as Ryan was concerned. He wondered if Johnny felt it too, the emotional distance that opened up along with the physical as soon as they'd come. Ryan itched to reach for Johnny, to kiss him again, to smooth over the cracks by touching him. But they were done for tonight, and Ryan needed to leave. "When do you want to meet next?" he asked.

"Tuesday maybe, or Wednesday?" Johnny said.

"Tuesday," Ryan replied quickly, and if he sounded too keen he didn't give a fuck. He needed something to look forward to between all the studying he'd be doing.

"Cool. It will have to be later again because of work. Nine-ish?"

"That's fine. See you then." Ryan gave Johnny a chaste kiss on the cheek, wanting to hug him tightly, wishing he could stay longer.

WHEN HE GOT BACK to his place, Ryan found Ewan alone in the living room. He was sitting on the sofa with revision notes, but the TV was on and Ewan seemed to be more focused on an old episode of *Friends* than he was on his work.

"Multitasking?" Ryan asked, sitting down beside him.

"Yeah." Ewan gave him a guilty grin. "God I'll be glad when these exams are over. Have you been out? Not revising tonight?"

"Yeah, I just went next door for a bit."

"How's that going?" Ewan's voice was casual, his gaze on the TV rather than Ryan.

Ryan sighed heavily. "I dunno really."

Ewan turned to look at him then. "Not great? I thought you seemed a bit off on Friday night."

"Yeah, sorry I was a bit pissy with you."

"Well it's none of my business, and I know I'm prone to being nosey, but if you want to talk then Uncle Ewan is always here for you."

Ryan laughed. "I'm imagining you in a floral armchair in 1970s slacks like some kind of TV agony uncle." He paused, turning serious again. Ewan might be nosey but he was a good listener and usually gave sound advice. "Actually, yeah. Maybe I could use your input. Not here though. My room?" He didn't want to risk being overheard by the others.

"Okay." Ewan turned the TV off and abandoned his notes on the coffee table.

Upstairs, Ryan shut the door behind them and they sat on the bed—Ryan leaning against the headboard while Ewan sat cross-legged at the foot.

"So, what's up?" Ewan raised his eyebrows.

Feeling faintly foolish now he was faced with Ewan's expectant face, Ryan wasn't sure where to begin.

"Well... this thing with Johnny, it's only supposed to be casual. But I think maybe I'm getting a bit attached to him. Like... it's just sex, I mean that's all we do together. We went on a sort of date once, but since then it's purely fucking and fooling around. And we agreed that it wasn't exclusive and I thought I was okay with that. But then on Friday night I saw another guy leaving his place and it was obviously a guy he'd hooked up with, and I didn't like knowing he'd been with someone else."

"Have you talked to him about it?"

"No." Ryan sighed. "I thought about it but wasn't sure what to say. He tried to bring it up too, but I shut him down and told him I'm fine with things as they are."

"But you aren't."

"No. Not really."

"Well you're going to have to tell him that. Otherwise you're just going to carry on feeling resentful if he carries on meeting other guys. If he doesn't know how you feel then nothing's going to change."

"But I don't think it's fair for me to ask him to be exclusive."

"Why not?" Ewan's brows lowered in confusion. "It's not unreasonable if you're seeing someone regularly to suggest that. He might say no, and want to keep things casual, in which case you have to think again about whether you can handle it or not. But he might agree to giving it a try."

"But I don't want a relationship with him. I don't think I'm ready for more than what we're doing already."

"Oh." Understanding dawned. "So you only want to fuck him, not date him, or hang out with him, but you don't want anyone else to have him?"

Ryan squirmed at the judgement on Ewan's face. "Basically, yes." Ryan flushed. "I know it sounds shitty, but that's where I'm at with it. And wanting that already makes me a wanker, but at least I'm definitely not enough of a wanker to actually *ask* for that. That counts for something, right?"

Ewan rolled his eyes. "I suppose. And yeah, you can't ask that unless you want Johnny to tell you where to stick it —and it won't be inside him anymore."

"Exactly."

"Am I right in thinking that a big part of this is you not wanting to come out as bi?"

There was no way Ryan could wriggle away from the question when it was asked so directly. Cheeks flaming, he admitted, "Yeah. But you know I'm not homophobic. I've never had a problem with you and Dev, or any of the guys next door. I've always been an ally."

"There's more than one kind of homophobia," Ewan said gently. "Internalised homophobia can be one of the biggest giants to fight." There was sympathy on his face as Ewan added, "Ryan, if you're bi, you're not an ally. You're one of us whether you like it or not. But only you can decide whether to step out of the closet, and only you can decide whether what you've got going on with Johnny is worth trying to hang on to."

"I don't think Johnny wants a relationship anyway." Ryan deflected. Ewan's words had hit home, but he'd deal with the fallout later. "He seems completely averse to commitment."

Ewan shrugged. "Well, you won't find out for sure unless you ask him."

"I guess."

They stared at each other, and there was nothing left to say.

"Okay, well I'll leave you to work it out. If you want to talk again, you know where I am." Ewan got up and stretched. "I'm going to bed now. Night, man."

"Night," Ryan replied. "Oh, and Ewan? Thanks. You've given me a lot to think about."

"You're welcome."

FOURTEEN

After Ryan left on Sunday night, Johnny showered, and then watched a crappy horror movie on Netflix while he waited to get sleepy. His phone buzzed with a few Grindr notifications but he ignored them at first. Following his experience with Carl and his subsequent guilt, he had no great urge to try and hook up with anyone else at the moment.

A little later, after a few more notifications had flashed up on his screen he gave in to curiosity and opened the app. One message was from Carl, asking if he wanted to meet again. Johnny replied with: *no thanks, man. I'm not looking for anything regular*.

Carl sent back: *no worries*, and Johnny deleted the message thread.

He had a few messages from new guys. Mostly the ubiquitous *Hey*, and a couple that came with bonus dick pics. Johnny deleted them all without replying and closed the app. He let his finger hover over the icon, considering deleting the app itself. But then he remembered Ryan's insistence that he was fine with things as they were:

It's not like this is serious.
It's just fucking.

Those words had stung, even though Johnny should have been relieved to hear them in some ways. It made life easier, nothing needed to change.

Leaving the app as it was, Johnny locked his phone, and set it aside. Maybe he'd be in the mood to find someone else to play with again soon, and if not, that was his problem. He didn't need to admit to Ryan that he'd temporarily ruined him for other guys. That could be Johnny's secret, and hopefully he'd get over it when the novelty wore off—or he'd deal with it when Ryan got bored of Johnny and moved on, whichever happened first.

"HI, HOW ARE YOU?" Johnny asked as he opened the door to Ryan on Tuesday evening.

"Knackered." Ryan gave a rueful smile. "Too much studying. My brain hurts. How are you?"

Johnny led the way upstairs. "I'm knackered as well. Long day at work. I got called in early to cover for someone who was sick so I was there for eleven hours instead of my usual eight-hour shift."

"Sounds tiring."

"Yeah, it was busy today too. I was on the till for hours, and then there was a huge delivery to unpack."

They were in Johnny's room now and Ryan closed the door behind them. He yawned loudly then said, "Oh God, sorry. It's nothing personal. I told you I was knackered."

Johnny chuckled. "No offence taken. I almost texted to cancel earlier." It had crossed his mind during his afternoon break. He was already exhausted and irritable and had fleetingly wondered whether he wouldn't rather just get home and go straight to bed. But then he'd remembered how good being with Ryan made him feel, and he reckoned he'd sleep better after a good shag.

"I'm glad you didn't," Ryan said, advancing on him. "I've been looking forward to this all day."

"Yeah?" Johnny gave his wickedest grin, dipping his head flirtatiously, and letting his hair fall over one eye.

"Yeah." Ryan cupped Johnny's cheek and kissed his lips, tucking the stray blond strand behind Johnny's ear.

They kissed for a while. It was slow and gentle tonight rather than their usual zero-to-sixty of sexual arousal, perhaps because they were both so tired. Then Ryan moved his lips to Johnny's cheek and down to his neck before he sighed, wrapping his arms around Johnny and settling into a hug. Enjoying the rare moment of intimacy that was comforting rather than sexual, Johnny put his arms around Ryan's waist, holding him close. Ryan slid his hands slowly down Johnny's back, from his shoulder blades to the curve at the base of his spine. Johnny arched into his touch like a cat. Ryan ran them back up, and then down again with firmer pressure, rubbing over Johnny's muscles that were tired from him being on his feet all day.

"Mmm," Johnny hugged him tighter.

"You like that?" Ryan repeated the movement.

"Yeah. It's good."

"You got any massage oil?"

"Uh. I don't think so, but I've got cocoa butter lotion in the bathroom." Johnny used it on dry skin. He liked the sweet scent of it. He lifted his head off Ryan's shoulder and smiled. "You gonna give me a massage? I'll do you after if you want."

"Yeah, that would be awesome."

Johnny detached himself to get the lotion. When he returned, Ryan had stripped down to his boxer briefs and was sitting on the edge of the bed. "Strip off, and come and lie down."

Johnny took off everything apart from his underwear—skimpy powder-blue briefs today, but men's ones, not women's. "These too?"

Ryan's gaze scanned approvingly over them. "They're sexy, but yes. I don't want to get lotion on them."

"Okay." After slipping them off, Johnny pushed the duvet down, climbed onto the bed, and lay face down, his head pillowed on his arms. He closed his eyes and felt the dip of the bed as Ryan moved to kneel astride him.

The first glide of Ryan's hands was cool, but the lotion warmed quickly on Johnny's skin. Ryan started with Johnny's shoulders, kneading the muscles gently at first. "That okay?" Ryan asked.

"Yeah. But you can go harder if you want."

Ryan snorted. "Always happy to oblige on that front."

"Haha," Johnny said, too relaxed already to come up with a better retort. He hummed a sound of pleasure as Ryan rubbed his muscles more firmly, his thumbs pressing in just right. "Damn that's good."

Ryan massaged him in silence, gradually working his way lower down Johnny's back, kneading out the tension either side of his spine and in the small of his back. The touch of his hands sparked a slow, lazy arousal; delicious, warm syrup in the pit of Johnny's belly. As Ryan squeezed his arse, Johnny gave a little moan, pressing his erection into the bed.

Ryan chuckled. "Good?"

"Amazing."

Ryan trailed his thumbs down Johnny's crack and Johnny couldn't resist tilting his hips up, wordlessly begging for more. Ryan shifted, kneeing Johnny's thighs apart so he could fit between them as he massaged the muscles in Johnny's butt cheeks, deliberately dipping in to graze over his hole with the tip of his thumbs. "Want me to fuck you?" he asked.

Biting back the urge to say yes, Johnny decided against instant gratification. This was too good, and once they both came Ryan would leave and it would be over. "Not yet," he said instead. "I want to give you a massage first."

"Now?"

"Yeah, let's swap." Johnny knelt up and turned, sliding his arms around Ryan and kissing him. Ryan's cock was hard in his boxer briefs and Johnny reached down to line his up against it and grind for a moment before pulling away. "Okay, your turn."

Ryan lay down on his front, and Johnny straddled his hips and squirted some lotion onto Ryan's back. "It looks like I've come all over you," he said, amused. He smeared the pale streaks, rubbing them into Ryan's skin. "This rubs in better though. Jizz would be no good as massage oil." He focused on Ryan's shoulders, kneading the powerful muscles there, seeking out knots and tension with his thumbs.

Ryan groaned. "God that feels amazing."

"Yeah?" Johnny carried on, repeating the rhythmic movements, and putting as much power behind it as he could. As he leaned forward to use his bodyweight, his cock rubbed over Ryan's arse, leaving a smear of precome on his underwear. "Can I take these off?" He pinged the elastic at the waist.

"Sure." Ryan lifted his hips so Johnny could pull them down and off.

Settling back into his previous position, Johnny carried on working on Ryan's shoulders. Without Ryan's underwear in the way Johnny's dick rested naturally in the groove of Ryan's arse crack, half-hard and sliding lazily back and forth as he moved his hands in circular movements from Ryan's shoulder blades up to his shoulders, out, and back around. It felt good, and he got harder again, his cock pressing more insistently against Ryan's arse.

"You having fun back there?" Ryan asked, craning to look over his shoulder at Johnny.

"A little bit." Johnny grinned. "Is it okay? I don't want to freak you out."

"Well I'm assuming you're not going to stick it in me with no lube, no condom, and no warning. So yeah, it's okay." Ryan settled back down, his face hidden in the crook of his arms, and then added, "It feels pretty hot actually."

Permission granted, Johnny carried on, precome starting to slick the way as he thrust more deliberately. His imagination took over and a vivid fantasy of spreading Ryan's cheeks apart and sliding into him filled Johnny's mind. He remembered how Ryan had lost himself in sensation when Johnny had fingered him, how he'd fallen apart, clenching around Johnny's fingers. The thought of Ryan doing that on his cock was almost too much. "God, I'd love to fuck you," he muttered. "I'd love to spread your legs and put my cock inside you."

Ryan tensed, buttocks clenching. The exact opposite of what Johnny had in mind. "I'm not ready for that."

Johnny stilled his hips. "I know, sorry. It was just fantasy. I know you don't want to do it. That's okay. I like you fucking me. I love you fucking me. We can stick to that."

"Maybe one day," Ryan said. "Just... not yet. But you could use your fingers in me again."

"Now?" Johnny ran his hands down Ryan's back to squeeze his glutes.

"If you like?"

"Yeah. Can I blow you while I do it?"

"Not gonna say no to that." Ryan raised his head, smiling, and relaxed again. "How about we sixty-nine and finger each other?"

"Fuck, yes. Let's do that."

They rearranged themselves, Johnny on his back and Ryan kneeling over him, and they started sucking each other off and stroking each other's holes with lube-slick fingers. Johnny moaned as Ryan slipped one into him, immediately ramping up the pleasure and intensity. He circled Ryan's hole a few times, assessing how easy it was going to be before gently pressing inside. Ryan was tight, and he groaned as Johnny's finger slid in. "Okay?" Johnny pulled off to ask.

"Yeah," Ryan managed breathlessly, and then his mouth was back on Johnny's cock, sucking enthusiastically.

After that it was a tangled build of mutual arousal, the wet sounds of mouths, dicks, and lubed fingers, punctuated by moans and stifled grunts. Johnny was close, but he wanted to make Ryan come before he let go, so tugged on Ryan's hip with his free hand, encouraging him to fuck Johnny's mouth. Ryan obliged, his cock hitting the back of Johnny's throat as he thrust. Johnny fingerfucked him in time, curling to reach Ryan's prostate. *Please come soon, please come soon. I can't hold out much longer.*

Ryan was groaning now, his sounds getting louder until

finally Johnny was rewarded by the throb of Ryan's cock and the first warm pulse of come. Johnny spiralled into blissful release, sucking and swallowing the rest of Ryan's load as he started to come too. Ryan choked and pulled off, wrapping a hand around Johnny's cock instead to stroke, then gave a surprised bark of laughter.

When they were both finished, Johnny let Ryan's cock slip free from his mouth. "You okay down there?"

"I need to work on my swallowing. I nearly got jizz in my eye." Ryan turned around and knelt beside Johnny. "Look at the state of me."

Come painted Ryan's cheek on one side, from just below his eye down to his jaw.

Johnny chuckled, and Ryan started laughing again too. Johnny found he couldn't stop, high on orgasm and the sight of Ryan's amused outrage. The more he laughed, the more Ryan did.

"It's a good thing you didn't get it in your eye," Johnny finally managed, still weak from his laughing fit. "Been there, done that. It stings like a bitch and makes your eye get really red."

"Seriously?" Ryan reached for a tissue and started to wipe his face clean.

"Yeah. Come here, you missed a bit."

Ryan lay down beside Johnny, and Johnny wiped the last bit of come from his chin where it was caught in his stubble. "You might be a bit flaky later but that's the worst of it." He kissed Ryan on the mouth, lightly at first until Ryan kissed him back, parting his lips, and pulling Johnny into his arms. They made out for a while, sweet and lazy, and Johnny wished he knew what was going through Ryan's head. This felt so tender, so intimate. Surely these feelings couldn't be as one-sided as he feared. Ryan touched him as if he was something precious, something that mattered, *someone* who mattered, not just a casual fuck buddy. He shivered, skin cooling now, and reached to tug the duvet up over them without breaking the kiss. In the warm cocoon of his bed, with Ryan wrapped around him, it was easy to believe this could turn into something. Maybe if they carried on, they'd end up on the same page eventually. Johnny certainly wasn't ready to give up hope.

FIFTEEN

At some point the kissing slowed, becoming gentle presses of lips on lips, then on cheeks, necks, and shoulders. Ryan knew he should probably leave now, but warm and comfortable and loving the intimacy of their contact, he had no desire to go.

Johnny settled with his head on Ryan's shoulder, drawing ticklish circles on Ryan's chest with his fingertips. Ryan breathed in the scent of his silky hair and tried to deal with the ache of longing that was building in his chest. It swelled and grew, stealing space in his lungs until he knew he couldn't contain it anymore. Surely Johnny had to feel something for him? The bond between them was tangible. Although it was based very much on the physical there was already more to this than sexual attraction, there was vulnerability and trust, and Ryan believed there was the potential for so much more.

But it had to begin with honesty.

He had to tell Johnny about his feelings, even if he didn't know exactly what he wanted to come of them. As Johnny's weight grew heavier and his breathing changed, signalling sleep, Ryan started planning the words he needed to say. Johnny dozing off gave him the time he needed to work out how to broach the subject. If Johnny would agree to be exclusive, to make this into something more official, then surely he would be prepared to give Ryan time to adjust. He didn't have to come out to everyone immediately, make a big announcement. They could start with telling a few friends first and take it from there. One step at a time.

The weight in Ryan's chest lifted with the decision made. He was ready to be honest. If Johnny didn't want more, that would hurt, but at least he'd know. Ryan couldn't deal with the uncertainty anymore and it had to be better to get things out in the open. He tightened his arms around Johnny, fear and excitement warring at the thought of the possible outcomes. He risked losing Johnny completely if he didn't feel the same, but he couldn't carry on like this. When Johnny woke, he'd tell him how he felt. But for now he was going to enjoy this moment in case it was the last time he got to hold Johnny like this. The thought of that was like the twist of a knife in his stomach. His eyelids felt heavy, so he closed them, giving into the urge to doze—just for a little while.

RYAN JERKED awake at the chime of a phone. It wasn't an alert tone that he recognised. He lifted his head and opened his eyes to darkness and heard the sound of deep, slow breathing beside him. Ryan could feel the warmth of another body. As the fog of sleep lifted, he realised he must still be in Johnny's bed.

"Johnny?" he whispered.

The rhythm of Johnny's breathing remained steady. He was lost in a sleep so deep Ryan would have to shake him to get a reaction. Maybe Ryan should get up and go home, but the light by the bed had still been on when Ryan fell asleep, so Johnny must have woken at some point and turned it off. He'd let Ryan stay, so was presumably okay with him sleeping there. Ryan didn't want to move, and he still needed to talk to Johnny. He let his head fall back on the pillow and closed his eyes.

They could talk in the morning.

As he was drifting back into sleep, the phone chimed again.

With a huff of irritation, Ryan sat up, making the bed springs creak. "Johnny?" he said a little louder. "Want to turn the sound off on your phone?"

Johnny stirred and made a snuffling sound, but nothing intelligible.

The phone chimed again.

Casting his gaze around the room, Ryan spotted the glow of the screen on Johnny's desk. He got up and carefully picked his way through Johnny's room in the darkness. Luckily Johnny had an iPhone like Ryan, so it would be easy enough for Ryan to flip the switch to put it on silent. As he reached out to pick up the phone he noticed it was nearly two in the morning. Then he saw the notifications on the screen and his stomach lurched.

Three of them. All from Grindr, telling Johnny he had a message.

It wasn't as if Ryan didn't know they weren't exclusive. Hell, on Sunday he'd basically given Johnny his blessing when they'd had that stupid abortive conversation up on the Hoe, because he hadn't had the balls to be honest. But seeing the evidence in front of him again hurt. Just because Johnny was technically allowed to hook up with other people, it didn't make Ryan feel any better about it.

Surely if Johnny had feelings for Ryan he wouldn't be hooking up with randoms just because he could? There was no way he could feel the same as Ryan did.

Cursing his stupidity for getting his hopes up, Ryan crept around in the darkness, gathering his clothes, and dressing as silently as he could.

Once he was dressed, Ryan stood for a moment and listened to the soft sound of Johnny's breathing, rising and falling like gentle waves lapping the shore. His heart was a heavy weight and emotion formed a tangled ball of regret, anger, and humiliation in his belly. He'd been stupid to think this was more than casual fucking. Thank goodness he hadn't tried to ask Johnny for more; that conversation would only have ended in disappointment and Ryan didn't think he could have handled Johnny letting him down gently. Ryan's eyes burned and he blinked, trying to force back the tears that threatened.

He left, treading softly over the threshold before pulling the door closed behind him with the barest of clicks. The stairs creaked as he made his way down but other than that, the house was silent. Tension left him in a whoosh of breath as he finally stepped out into the night. Rain was falling hard and the street was slick and shiny with puddles. Pausing on the street between their two houses, Ryan looked up into the blackness of the sky and let the rain fall on his face. As the rainwater trickled down his cheeks it was hard to tell whether any tears escaped to keep it company. He stood until his clothes were soaked through and his teeth were chattering, only then did he go and let himself into his house.

In his room, Ryan stripped down to his boxer briefs and crawled into the refuge of his bed. He shivered, locked in physical misery to match his distress. Willing his mind to empty he tried to breathe slowly, counting his breath backwards from 100 until he got to zero, and then started all over again. He got to zero four times before his shivers stopped and he fell into a thankfully dreamless sleep at last.

THE NEXT MORNING, Ryan woke early and briefly experienced that moment of peace between sleeping and waking before the memory of the night before lurched into his consciousness like an unwelcome drunk at a party demanding attention. The evening had been so perfect, until….

"Ugh." Ryan curled in on himself, stomach clenched with anxiety and unhappiness.

Like he didn't already have enough to be stressed about with his exams less than a week away. The last thing he needed was to be constantly thinking about Johnny. He needed a clean break, to draw a line under everything that had happened between them and move on. Better to get out now before he got even deeper. Better to keep his focus on his studying, on his future. Johnny wasn't going to be part of that and Ryan obviously couldn't handle the distraction. What had started as a fun diversion had become a source of stress; Ryan needed to take responsibility and walk away.

He forced himself out of bed and into the shower, then down to the kitchen where he managed to eat some toast even though it felt like cardboard in his mouth and his stomach protested at the invasion. Two cups of coffee banished the sleep fog from his brain and he went back up to his room ready to concentrate on work.

The sound of a text alert broke his focus after a couple of hours, but he ignored it, pushing on with the facts he was cramming until his phone buzzed again ten minutes later.

Looking at his screen, Ryan ignored the little flip of his heart as he read the words from Johnny:

Last night was great :) hope you slept well x

Then the second message:

Are you okay this morning?

As he looked, a third pinged in:

Want to meet again soon? Let me know. I'm working late today but you could come over after nine.

It was so tempting to say yes, to go and indulge in the inevitable physical pleasure of whatever the evening would bring. But no. Steeling himself, Ryan typed:

Sorry, not tonight. I'm behind on revision and need to catch up.

It wasn't entirely a lie. There was always more he could do, and Johnny had been a distraction recently.

No worries. Good luck with that. Maybe tomorrow then?

Ryan hesitated. Maybe he should end it now, tell Johnny he was done. But telling him by text rather than face-to-face seemed like a dick move. So he replied with: *Maybe. I'll let you know.*

Okay x

Ryan didn't feel bad about being evasive. It wasn't like Johnny was going to be short of company. He could hook up with one of his Grindr buddies after all. He sighed and set his phone aside, and then turned back to his revision.

ON THURSDAY AFTERNOON Johnny looked back at the message thread on his phone. Ryan had said he'd let Johnny know about tonight but hadn't been in contact since. At first Johnny hadn't worried. He'd been working the last two days so hadn't had much time to dwell, and he knew

Ryan was busy with studying for his exams. But now doubts were creeping in.

Ryan had left on Tuesday night without waking him. After the intimacy of the evening that seemed a little odd. Johnny thought Ryan would have at least been the sort to leave a note, or text, for him to wake up to. He re-read the messages. It was hard to judge the tone but Ryan had been quite short, not chatty, and hadn't added any smiles or kisses. But again, maybe he was just busy and stressed and Johnny was reading too much into his lack of enthusiasm.

Feeling lonely and fed up, Johnny stayed up late watching Netflix in bed that night. It was only when he got a Grindr message notification that he realised his normal default on a night like that would have been to hook up, but it hadn't even occurred to him. He'd been ignoring messages since he'd met Carl, and he didn't bother to open this message either. Instead, he jerked off thinking about Ryan and lay awake feeling unsettled. Maybe he should try to talk to Ryan again, but his last attempt at a serious conversation hadn't gone well. And with Ryan's exams approaching, now probably wasn't the best time. He'd sit tight and see how things felt after Ryan's exams were over.

BY THE TIME he left work on Friday, Johnny was in a terrible mood. The shop had been busy and he'd had more than his fair share of arsehole customers for one day. Despite being run off his feet, he'd spent way too much time obsessing over Ryan and the lack of contact, which only made him more fed up. He'd nearly lost his shit with the last twat of a customer who'd tried to return something that had obviously been worn on a night out around smokers and then yelled at Johnny when he refused to accept it back.

Fortunately Johnny's manager had intervened and saved him from saying something that might have cost him his job.

To make matters worse, it was raining again—the weather had been awful this week—and it was too windy for an umbrella. Johnny didn't wear sensible things like raincoats or hats, so by the time he turned the corner into his street his hair was plastered to his head, his skinny jeans clung to his legs like a second skin, and water was trickling unpleasantly down the back of his neck.

All in all, it was the worst possible timing for him to literally bump into Ryan who was running in the opposite direction.

Heads down against the wind and rain, they didn't see each other till it was too late. Johnny caught a flash of Ryan's surprised expression as he rounded the corner before they collided. Throwing his arms up instinctively, Johnny grabbed Ryan's biceps to hold himself upright.

"Shit. Sorry!" Ryan gasped breathlessly.

"Fucking hell. You nearly knocked me over." Johnny regained his balance, but kept his hands on Ryan's arms. His muscles were thick and solid beneath the thin compression top he was wearing under a short-sleeved layer. Hoping that maybe this would be a turning point in his shitty day, Johnny grinned at Ryan. "So, how are you? I've missed you."

Ryan's gaze slid away from Johnny's eyes evasively and he stepped back, lifting a hand to wipe a curl of wet hair off his forehead. "Not bad thanks, busy... you know. Just out for a run."

"So I see," Johnny said, acid creeping into his tone at Ryan's coldness. "Well don't let me stop you." He didn't mean to sound bitchy, but he couldn't help it. This sudden distance between them was hurtful. He knew Ryan needed to focus on his exams, but with Ryan right in front of him and barely able to look him in the eye, the avoidance felt personal as well as practical. Something had changed and Johnny didn't know what, or why. He couldn't resist pushing. "Am I right in assuming you won't want to hook up this weekend? Revision taking priority again?"

"Yeah. Um...." Ryan flicked his eyes up to meet Johnny's for a moment and the regret in them was stark. It hit Johnny like a punch in the gut because he knew what was coming. "Actually I think it's best if we just leave it. Stop seeing each other. It's been fun, but it's too much of a distraction... meeting so often. So can we call it a day?"

The icy chill down Johnny's spine was nothing to do with the rainwater now. He didn't know why Ryan had turned it into a question, when his mind was clearly made up.

"Of course." Johnny shrugged, his voice curt. "If that's what you want."

Ryan stared at him, looking pretty fucking miserable for the person who was doing the dumping. "I think it's best. Feels like it was taking up too much of our time for something that was supposed to be casual, and neither of us wants anything serious, do we?"

Again with the questions. If Ryan had asked Johnny what he wanted *before* he'd told him he wanted to break up, then Johnny might have been honest. But now his pride made him reply quickly, "Yeah, no. Course not. We knew that from the start."

Ryan seemed to be searching Johnny's face for something, and Johnny hoped his emotions weren't showing because on the inside he was crumbling.

Hurt, rejection, humiliation, misery.

This was why he'd avoided relationships for so long,

because these feelings were unbearable. Johnny had spent so long protecting himself from them but Ryan had broken through his defences. Using the last bit of his willpower, Johnny fought down the wave of unwelcome emotion and said, "Well, I wanna get out of the rain because it's fucking horrible out here. So I'll see you around, I guess. Good luck with the exams." And with that he shoved his hands in his pockets so he wouldn't be tempted to try to touch Ryan, and hurried past him to walk away without looking back.

SIXTEEN

The brain's capacity for avoiding unpleasant thoughts was nothing short of a miracle, and was the only thing that got Ryan through the next few days. He buried his emotions and turned himself into a robot, going through the motions of self-care and study. Sleep, eat, revise, run. His days were ruthlessly organised with no time to spare on brooding. He thought he was doing a good job of acting like nothing was wrong, and at first he got away with it. Tied up with their own exam stress, his housemates were distracted, and their thoughts were turned inwards. But on the night before his first exam, Ryan went to the gym with Ewan in the evening, and on their way home they met Johnny in the street, obviously on his way out somewhere.

He looked breathtaking, blond hair tangled in a way that made Ryan want to twine his fingers into it, and eyes ringed with even more black eyeliner than usual. He was dressed all in black and the sight of his long legs made Ryan feel weak. With his phone in hand, Johnny only looked up when Ewan greeted him.

"Hi, Johnny. How's things?"

"Not bad thanks." Johnny's gaze slid to Ryan.

Ryan gave an awkward nod. "Hey."

Johnny's phone chimed and he looked down at the screen again before pocketing it. There was an awkward silence. Ryan knew Ewan was expecting him to say something, but his tongue felt like it was coated in glue as he stared hopelessly at Johnny wondering where he was going and who he was on his way to meet.

"Off out? Alright for some," Ewan said cheerfully. "Think of us poor final year students while you're out having fun."

"Oh I will," Johnny replied, but his tone was tense rather than amused. "Don't you worry. Better go. I'm late. See you around."

"Have a drink for me." Ewan patted Johnny on the shoulder as he passed on Ewan's side, avoiding any contact with Ryan.

"Will do."

Ryan resisted the urge to turn and watch him go.

"What the fuck, man?" Ewan asked as soon as they were inside. "What's going on with you two? You spoke one word, and he'd barely look you in the eye."

"I don't want to talk about it." Ryan walked to the kitchen, following the sound of voices. Nadia and Justine were in there cooking, and Ewan wouldn't ask about Johnny while they were there. He poured himself a glass of water at the sink and downed it, the cool liquid doing nothing to soothe the churning ache in his gut.

When he turned Ewan was standing behind him, hands on hips, and determination written in the set of his jaw. He raised his eyebrows.

"I'm going to shower." Ryan pushed past him.

But Ewan followed him upstairs. "What happened with

Johnny?" he asked as soon as they were out of earshot of the kitchen. "Did you talk to him?"

Reaching the landing, Ryan wheeled around, pissed off with Ewan's persistence. "I broke up with him, okay?" he snapped. "And like I said. I don't want to talk about it."

Ewan's eyes widened and his face fell. "Shit."

The anger left Ryan as quickly as it came, and he was suddenly overcome with bone-deep tiredness from pushing himself too hard physically and mentally. "Yeah. It is shit." He sagged where he stood, shoulders slumping.

Ewan opened the door to Ryan's room and gently guided him inside.

Ryan sat on the edge of his bed and leaned his elbows on his knees. He stared down at the carpet, eyes homing in on a slight stain where he'd spilled a cup of tea a few months ago. The mattress dipped and the bed creaked as Ewan sat beside him, then the warm weight of his hand landed between Ryan's shoulder blades. "I'm sorry, man."

Too exhausted to feel more than numb, Ryan sighed. "I'll get over it. It's not like it was serious. We'd only been seeing each other for a couple of weeks."

"Sometimes that's all it takes to get emotionally attached though. I should know. It didn't take long with Dev."

Maybe Ewan was trying to make him feel better, but the reminder of what he had with Dev only made Ryan feel worse. "Yeah, but Dev felt the same about you."

"And Johnny doesn't?"

"No."

Ryan couldn't be bothered to explain that he hadn't even asked Johnny how he felt. It was obvious. Johnny had never wanted to be exclusive, he'd been seeking other hook ups while he was involved with Ryan. And now, while

Ryan was nursing a heart that was bruised and battered—if not completely broken—Johnny was already out, presumably looking for his next conquest. Ryan had to accept that he was just another notch on Johnny's bedpost and that was all he was ever going to be.

"That sucks."

"Yep." Ryan heaved a huge sigh and raised his head. "But it is what it is, and I have more important things to worry about. Like my first exam tomorrow. Speaking of which, I really should get showered, fed, and do a bit of last minute revision before I try and sleep. When's your first exam?"

"Friday." Ewan grimaced. "Mine are all quite close together, which is good in some ways. But I just want to get started now, the waiting sucks." He stood and stretched. "Okay, man. I'll leave you to it. I'm sorry things didn't work out with Johnny though. But hey, at least you know you're into guys as well as girls now. Self-discovery is never a bad thing."

"Yeah." Ryan managed a weak smile. "I guess it's good to know I have options."

"YOU LOOK like someone pissed in your cornflakes this morning. What the hell is wrong with you?" Simon asked Johnny.

They were both on their lunchbreak. It was a bright, sunny day so they'd bought takeaway coffee and sandwiches and were sitting on a bench on the grassy, tree-lined space that ran down the centre of the shopping precinct.

Johnny shrugged. "I'm just tired. I was out late last night." He'd been miserable for the past week, ever since

Ryan had broken things off. He was doing his best to fuck Ryan out of his system but with no success at all. Hooking up with other guys only reinforced how different things had felt with Ryan. How much better. How richer the physical experience was when there was an emotional connection too.

"Did you have a good time?"

"Not really. I gave someone a blowjob in a club toilet but he fucked off as soon as he'd come. Selfish twat. If I'd known he wasn't going to reciprocate I'd have at least had a wank while I blew him."

"Oh I hate that," Simon said.

Ryan had always taken care of Johnny, always made sure that he had as much fun as Ryan did. He remembered the sensation of Ryan's mouth on his cock, his tongue on his arse, the thick thrust of him as he'd pressed kisses down Johnny's spine. He sighed; frustrated arousal shot through with longing that was almost too much to bear.

He glanced sideways and realised Simon was studying him curiously. "You sure you're just tired?"

"Yeah." Johnny liked Simon, but they weren't that close. Johnny wanted to preserve his image as the carefree Casanova. He was the one who broke hearts, not the other way around. The humiliation of being dumped was almost as bad as the pain. Maybe he should talk to someone though; dealing with it alone didn't seem to be going too well. There was only one person Johnny was prepared to bare his soul to.

As he and Simon walked back to the shop after their lunch break, Johnny got out his phone and sent Sid a text:

Hey. I could use an ear. You free to meet up one evening?

Sid replied as Johnny and Simon reached their workplace: *Tonight, or tomorrow?*

The signal wasn't always good indoors, so Johnny waved Simon ahead. "I'll catch you up, just need to reply to this."

Tonight's good. Johnny didn't want to go out and hook up again. Tea and sympathy from Sid sounded better than cider and non-reciprocal blowjobs from random strangers.

What do you want to do? My place? Your place? Go out for a drink?

Your place. Johnny wanted privacy for this conversation. Ben would probably be there, but that was okay. Ben might be a new friend rather than an old one like Sid, but he was a nice guy, kind, and a good listener.

Sure. Can you get here in time for dinner at 7ish? I promised Ben I'd make veggie fajitas and I can make enough for three.

Sounds lush. See you then.

IT FELT ODD TO JOHNNY, ringing the bell of the flat he used to live in with Sid. It was odder still to have Ben answer the door and invite Johnny into the place he used to call home.

"Hi, Johnny. Come in." Ben greeted him with a handshake that Johnny turned into a one-armed hug by pulling Ben closer, bottles in the supermarket carrier in Johnny's hand clinking against Ben's back.

"Hey, Ben, how's life in the love nest?" He smiled as he drew back.

Ben grinned, flushing. "It's good thanks."

"Haven't got fed up with him yet then? Found out all his bad habits now you're living together?"

"Nah. I can deal. Come on through, Sid's busy cooking. What do you want to drink?"

"I brought some fruit cider." Johnny held up the carrier bag. "I'll have one of these."

In the open plan kitchen/living area, the scent of spices and frying onions and garlic was thick in the air. Johnny's mouth watered and he realised he'd hardly eaten today. He hadn't had much of an appetite since he'd broken up with Ryan, but now the delicious scent made his stomach clench.

"Hey." He went up to look over Sid's shoulder. "That smells amazing."

"Hi." Sid put his wooden spoon down and turned to give Johnny a hug. "How are you?"

Johnny held on to him longer than he normally would. Sid's friendly embrace was comforting, and Johnny badly needed comfort. It was a week to the day since Ryan had called things off, and Johnny still didn't feel any better about it. He missed the contact with Ryan, the sex, the affection and closeness that had crept into their interactions. It wasn't as if they'd ever got to the point of a real relationship, but Johnny hadn't realised how much he'd been hoping for more until Ryan stripped that possibility away.

"Johnny?" Sid asked gently. "You okay?"

"Meh." Johnny pulled away reluctantly. "I've been better."

"Will cider help?" Ben offered him one of his bottles, now open.

"Maybe. Thanks." Johnny took it.

"Are you ready for a drink now, babe?" Ben asked.

"Yeah, lager please."

Ben got two bottles of San Miguel from the fridge and opened them for him and Sid.

Sid turned back to stir the onions and vegetables sizzling in a large pan. "So, what's up?"

"Can we eat first?" Johnny asked. He didn't want to

ruin his newfound appetite by getting miserable thinking about Ryan. "I'll tell you later."

"Sure."

"So, how are things with you? Is work going well? Saved any whales lately?" Johnny took a swig of his drink.

"Whales no, but I'm working on protecting some rare lichen."

Johnny laughed. "I guess somebody has to do it."

They talked about their jobs and Ben's studies while Sid finished cooking. Then over dinner—which tasted as good as it smelled—they got onto the topic of movies for a while. Johnny tried to relax and enjoy the conversation and he mostly managed it. But he was aware that he was more subdued than was usual for him, and he kept catching Sid looking at him. Ryan was at the back of Johnny's mind, a constant nagging itch that flared into a jolt of something more uncomfortable now and again.

Little things like Sid taking Ben's hand and holding it on the table once they'd finished eating, and the affectionate glances they exchanged, made Johnny's heart clench with an envy that was new. He'd never felt like this around happy couples before. After things had gone horribly awry with Craig, Johnny never wanted that kind of commitment again. Once he'd got over the pain of betrayal, he'd been relieved that he no longer craved that kind of attachment. He felt safe. With his no-strings barriers up nobody could hurt him. It wasn't like he was lonely or unfulfilled. He enjoyed the casual one-offs and the few fuck buddies he shared something regular with for a while. He hadn't noticed what he'd been missing until Ryan made him imagine what *more* might feel like. And now, with Sid and Ben's happiness right under his nose, Johnny felt an ache of longing.

"Anyone want some ice cream?" Ben asked.

"Nah. I'm good thanks." Johnny patted his stomach. He was full to bursting after a week of not eating enough.

"Not yet. I might have some later though." Sid started gathering their plates, so Johnny helped him clear the table while Ben scooped himself out a generous portion of ice cream.

A fresh drink in his hand, Johnny took a seat in the armchair, leaving the sofa for Ben and Sid.

"So?" Sid raised his eyebrows. "What's up?"

Johnny clutched the bottle in his hands tightly. "Ryan broke up with me."

"Wait, what? I didn't think you were dating him?" Sid frowned. "You said you were just fuck buddies. I didn't think you were serious about him."

"Dating, hooking up...." Johnny waved his free hand vaguely. "Whatever it was, it's over now, and I feel shitty about it. So I guess I was more serious about him than I thought."

"Did he finish it?" Ben asked.

"Yeah." Johnny drew his knees up, curling into the comfort of the saggy armchair.

"I'm sorry. Did he say why?" Sid's voice was sympathetic and it only made Johnny feel worse.

"That it was too much of a distraction. He's got exams and stuff and we were seeing too much of each other." Saying it aloud was painful, each word a twist of the knife. Johnny had spent the last four years making sure he would never feel disposable again, yet here he was. He was a fucking idiot and should have trusted his instincts and got out as soon as he started to have feelings for Ryan.

"That sucks. But maybe you can pick it up again once he's through his exams?" Ben suggested.

Johnny gave a huff of bitter amusement. "I think that was just his way of letting me down gently. It was never going to turn into anything serious. He barely put more than a toe out of the closet. He was only experimenting with me, which is fine because that was the deal. It was supposed to just be sex for me too."

"But you ended up wanting more." Sid's gaze was intent.

Johnny looked down at his bottle, reading the label without taking in the words. "Yeah. I guess."

There was a long silence.

"You know what though," Sid said cautiously. "You might be feeling like crap now, but actually maybe it's not a bad thing that this happened."

"Why?"

"Because you've been avoiding any kind of intimacy as long as I've known you, and it's not healthy. You say you don't care about relationships and you want to be single, but is that really true? I think you're just scared of being hurt because of what that arsehole Craig did to you. So you haven't let yourself fall for anyone since."

Johnny couldn't deny it was true. "Yeah, okay. So in an ideal world I suppose I would like a relationship. I see what you guys have and it makes me realise what I'm missing. But how is my unrequited crush on Ryan anything other than a bad thing? Feeling crap all over again is only going to make me more determined to avoid this in future. Being single might have its drawbacks, but at least it's a steady state of being okay. It's better than risking *this* every time I meet someone new."

"It's a good thing because it shows you're capable of feeling like this."

Johnny snorted. "What, before this you thought I was

dead inside? I'm not broken, Sid. I'm just cynical and pessimistic as fuck when it comes to relationships. And I'm still not sure it's worth getting on the rollercoaster. The highs might be great, but the lows are shitty."

"I used to think that too," Ben said. His voice sounded husky, and his cheeks flushed as they both turned to look at him. "For a long time I couldn't imagine ever taking that risk. Being transgender, it just seemed like way too much hassle to even try to date; there was way too much potential for rejection. But I'm glad I took a chance." He glanced sideways at Sid and gave a small smile. "The thing is, most people don't get happy-ever-afters. That's not how life works. Going into any relationship you always know that chances are it won't last forever. People usually have more than one significant relationship in their life, and some have many. And break-ups are hard, but that doesn't always mean the relationship wasn't one worth having while it lasted. I don't regret the relationship with my ex. He was important to me at the time, and I still have some good memories of that even though ultimately it didn't work out."

Johnny considered Ben's words for a moment. "So you're saying you reckon it's better to have something than nothing?"

"Better to have loved and lost?" Sid chipped in. "Like the old saying goes."

"Yeah." Ben shrugged. "It's a cliché maybe, but the old adages sometimes have some truth in them, and that one works for me. Even if it doesn't work out with us long term, I can't imagine ever regretting getting involved with you." He let his gaze slide to Sid and smiled.

Sid reached for Ben's hand and laced their fingers together.

"Yeah, well. Some relationships leave you with nothing

but regret, though," Johnny said bitterly. "I wish I'd never met Craig. The good times don't outweigh how much he hurt me. And what about people who are abused by their partners? I bet they usually wish they'd run a mile in the opposite direction when they met."

"Of course, I'm not saying every relationship is positive. Only that some are, even when they're transient. And personally I still think it's worth taking a chance in case it turns out to be amazing." Ben squeezed Sid's hand and Johnny felt it as an answering clench in his gut.

"Yeah. Maybe," Johnny conceded. Deep down he knew that if Ryan had wanted more from him, Johnny would have taken that risk. And perhaps in the future, if he met someone else who made him want more, then he'd take that chance with them.

But first he had to get over Ryan.

SEVENTEEN

One week later

JOHNNY OPENED the front door to the sound of music and chatter coming from the living room. He'd done a late shift at work today and it was nearly nine already. Starving on his way home, he'd stopped to buy some chips and had started eating while he walked. Thirsty from the salt, he went into the kitchen to get himself a drink. He finished his chips standing leaning against the kitchen counter and washed them down with a can of cider. Once he was done, he threw away the greasy paper, licked his fingers clean, and opened a second can.

Drink in hand, he hesitated in the hallway. He'd been really antisocial for the last week or so. Since his talk with Sid and Ben, he hadn't been out anywhere and had barely spoken to anyone outside work. Hooking up held no appeal at the moment. Even in the house he'd mostly stayed in his room, binge-watching anime, and feeling miserable. Hanging out with his housemates made him feel lonelier, because they were all part of happy couples and that bothered Johnny in a way it never had before.

He couldn't hide away forever though. It was Friday night. He had the day off tomorrow, and the first drink he'd chugged was already sending alcohol buzzing through his veins, making his spirits lift a little, if only temporarily.

Decision made, he pasted on a smile and walked in.

"Hey, guys."

The room was unusually crowded today. Every one of his housemates was present, along with Ewan who was sprawled in an armchair with Dev on his lap. Jez and Mac were on one sofa, and Shawn and Jude on the other. They all had drinks in their hands.

"Hey, Johnny. How are you?" Jez asked, while the others greeted him with assorted hi's, nods, and hand waves.

"Not bad thanks." Johnny took a seat on Jez and Mac's sofa. "You?"

"Good. Glad it's Friday."

"Wooooo!" Ewan waved his bottle of beer in the air. "And I finished my exams today. Thank *fuck*!" His speech was a little slurred. He'd obviously been celebrating for a while already.

"Oh cool. Bet you're glad they're over. How did they go?" Johnny took another sip of cider.

Ewan focused on Johnny as if he'd only just noticed he was there, brow furrowing a little. "Okay I think. I'll find out in July. Oh. That reminds me." He looked around at everyone. "Party at our place tomorrow night! We've all finished our exams now, so we're celebrating. You guys should come and party with us. It's gonna be awesome." He gestured with his bottle again, sloshing beer out onto Dev's knee.

"Careful, babe." Dev took the bottle and put it on the coffee table.

Johnny's stomach flipped at the thought of being at a party with Ryan again. That was how this whole mess had started. He couldn't imagine Ryan would be happy to see him. It was probably best if Johnny stayed away, but he was desperate to even catch a glimpse of him. He hadn't seen Ryan since they'd met in the street before his exams, and he wondered how he was doing. Did he miss Johnny at all?

"Do you know how Ryan's exams went?" he asked.

"What's it to you?" Ewan replied curtly.

Johnny stiffened at the belligerence in his voice. The atmosphere in the room was suddenly electric. The music playing was the only sound as the others turned as one to look at Johnny. He felt the weight of their stares like a heavy net, trapping him. "I just wondered. There's no need to be a dick about it."

"Yeah. Well if he did okay in his exams it's no thanks to you." Ewan glared at Johnny, his usually friendly face hostile and cold.

"Ewan, don't," Dev said, concerned. "Stay out of it."

"Yeah. Fuck you, man. Listen to your boyfriend. Because you obviously don't know what the hell you're talking about," Johnny snapped.

"You're not still seeing Ryan then?" Jez asked. "I thought maybe he hadn't been round because of the exams."

"No. They broke up, right before the exams started," Ewan said coldly. "Perfect timing huh?"

"Yes, but Ryan was the one who finished it!" Johnny's voice rose in outrage. Everyone was staring at him like he was shit on a shoe and it was totally unjustified. "He broke it off because I was too much of a distraction, apparently."

He spat the words out like bitter liquid. "It wasn't my choice!"

"He broke it off because he had feelings for you, and he wanted more than just sex, and you didn't feel the same," Ewan said. Anger had chased away the slur in his speech. Lucid and full of righteous indignation, his eyes were bright in his flushed face. "It messed him up, and he's been miserable ever since."

"What the hell?" Johnny gaped at Ewan. "That's not what happened at all. Seriously. If he had feelings for me he never fucking told me, and he certainly never asked me what I thought about it! And I'm pretty bloody miserable about it myself, so stop giving me a hard time when you don't know the facts."

There was a long pause while Johnny and Ewan locked gazes.

"Well if you're telling the truth then Ryan's an idiot," Ewan finally said, his face softening. "And maybe you're an idiot too for letting him go without being honest."

"I wanted to tell him. But he broke it off before I got the chance. There didn't seem any point telling him how I felt after that." Johnny's heart beat faster. "Are you sure he wanted more?"

Ewan nodded. "Yeah. I'm positive."

Johnny stared at him, finding it hard to believe what he was hearing. But Ewan wouldn't lie about something like this. It must be true. "Is Ryan in tonight?"

"No. He went out to the pub with James and Colin."

"Which pub?"

"The White Horse."

Johnny stood, hope surging, and adrenaline coursing through his veins. "I'm gonna go and find him."

"Yesssss!" Jez gave a fist pump.

"Go for it!" Jude said.

Johnny downed his can, needing the extra Dutch courage for what he was about to do. "Right." He looked around at the other guys, then let his gaze settle on Ewan. "If this goes horribly wrong I'm holding you responsible."

"I'll take that risk." Ewan grinned, then added, "Good luck, man."

"Thanks."

AS JOHNNY HALF-WALKED, half-ran all the way to The White Horse, he went over and over what he should say to Ryan in his head but it didn't help. When he arrived, breathless and sweating, his mind was a tangled mess. He was going to have to wing it.

Not giving himself time to chicken out, he burst straight through the doors and stepped into the noisy hustle and bustle of Friday night in a pub. It was very full. All the tables were taken and the bar was lined with people standing. He scanned the room for Ryan but couldn't see him anywhere. He made his way through the main bar and into the snug where he'd sat with Ryan before. There, he found Colin and James, but there was still no sign of Ryan.

"Is Ryan here?" Johnny demanded.

James and Colin looked up at him in surprise. "Oh. Hi, Johnny," Colin said.

Johnny didn't have the patience for social niceties. "Ryan. Where is he?"

"He went for a piss. What's up?" James frowned.

Johnny didn't bother replying. He was on a mission and couldn't be bothered to talk to anyone else. Wheeling around, he hurried back through the main bar to the toilets. Both urinals were occupied with men who weren't Ryan, but the cubicle door was ajar, and through it Johnny saw a familiar back view: broad shoulders and wavy brown hair that Johnny had felt slide between his fingers enough times to recognise it anywhere.

He slipped into the cubicle and locked the door shut behind him.

"HEY!" Ryan said indignantly at the sound of some idiot barging into the toilet cubicle behind him. He snapped his head around, expecting to see James pulling some stupid prank, and his eyes widened when he saw Johnny pulling the door shut and locking it.

What the hell? Why was he here?

The splattering sound of his urine hitting the seat instead of the water made him turn his attention back to the job in hand. He lowered his voice as he fixed his aim. "For fuck's sake, Johnny. I nearly pissed all over the floor."

"I don't think you'd be the first one to do that in here tonight."

He had a point. It wasn't exactly fresh in here. Ryan finished up, and turned around as he zipped himself up. "What the fuck are you doing here anyway?" His heart beat hard. Johnny looked nervous too, gaze intense as he stared at Ryan.

"I need to talk to you."

"What? Why? Here?"

"It's as good a place as any. We're alone, and nobody will overhear us as long as we're quiet."

"Okay." It might smell of piss, but Ryan sensed that Johnny didn't want to wait, and Ryan wanted to hear what he had to say. Crazy hope sparked in his chest but he tried to tamp it down, not wanting to be disappointed.

Johnny's words tumbled out fast. "I saw Ewan tonight and he had a go at me. He seemed to think that you broke up with me because you wanted more, but that I didn't feel the same. Why did he think that? It's bollocks and you know it. You never even asked me what I wanted. Why would you lie to Ewan?" He sounded angry and defensive, but that only added strength to the little flame burning in Ryan's chest.

"I didn't lie to him. I just assumed—"

"Ewan was right then."

"About what?"

"That you're an idiot." Johnny's voice rose. "For fuck's sake, Ryan. Did you really like me? I mean more-than-sex like me, and want more? Because if so, why didn't you tell me? Because I care about you too, and I was gutted when you broke things off."

Ryan gaped at him, trying to make sense of his words. Hope rose. Maybe they could fix this. "I was going to tell you," he admitted. "I'd decided to say something, and was hoping you felt the same. And then I saw loads of Grindr notifications on your phone that night when we fell asleep together. And I know we never said we'd be exclusive... but after that I couldn't bring myself to tell you how I felt. If you still wanted other people then we *didn't* feel the same, because I only wanted you."

"They were only messages, Ryan! I didn't meet anyone after that guy you saw me with—not while I was still seeing you. I didn't even reply to those messages you saw. If you'd asked me, I'd have told you I didn't want to hook up with other guys anymore. I know I said I didn't want anything serious at first, but being with you made me want more. I tried to talk to you about it, that day on the Hoe, remember? But you said it was just fucking, and I believed you."

Ryan winced as he remembered that conversation. He'd been hurt and angry and the lie had tripped out easily. But none of that was important anymore. It was all in the past and the only thing that mattered was the present. "So how do you feel about me now?" Ryan clenched his fists and his shoulders stiffened with tension as he waited.

Johnny stared at Ryan for a few seconds that felt too long, grey eyes wide, the eyeliner smudged around them, making his gaze even more intense. Finally he said, "I'm pissed off with you for being a dick and splitting up with me without talking to me first.... But I still like you. And I want us to give it another chance. A proper chance this time. With honesty on both sides."

Relief wrapped around Ryan like a warm blanket, his shoulders dropping as the tension began to trickle away. "And you don't want to see other people?"

"No. I want to be exclusive. So. What do you say—are you in?"

The warmth expanded into a bright rush of happiness. "Yes," Ryan said simply. Then he leaned forward and took Johnny's face in his hands, crowding him back up against the toilet door as he kissed him hard and deep and Johnny kissed him back, hands tight around Ryan's waist.

When they finally separated, they had to wait a few minutes for their erections to subside before they could leave the cubicle without embarrassment.

"I know you're not out to many people yet," Johnny said quietly as he leaned into Ryan's embrace. "And that's okay. But are you going to tell your housemates about me? Your mates waiting out there might be wondering what's going on with us."

"James already knew I'd been hooking up with you," Ryan said. "And yeah. I'll tell the rest of them."

Johnny's smile was radiant, and he kissed Ryan softly on the lips. "Good."

They finally emerged a few minutes later, flushed, and smiling like fools. A middle-aged man at the sinks did a double-take as they left the cubicle together, but he didn't comment. Ryan led the way back through the main bar with Johnny close behind. Every time their eyes met, they started grinning again.

"Hey," Ryan said as they got back to the table where James and Colin were sitting.

James gave Ryan a knowing grin, but Colin looked confused. "Is everything all right?" He glanced at Johnny warily, and then looked back at Ryan.

"Yeah." Ryan's heart surged as he reached for Johnny's hand and tugged him closer. Then he slipped his arm around Johnny's waist and smiled nervously. "Everything's fine now."

Colin's mouth dropped open while James's smile widened.

"For real?" James asked. "You two, you're a thing now... like properly?"

"Um. Yes. I guess?" Ryan glanced sideways at Johnny. "Are we a thing?"

Johnny laughed. "Yeah. I think we're a thing."

"A thing like what?" Colin asked. "Like boyfriends?"

Ryan raised his eyebrows questioningly at Johnny who shrugged and said, "Sounds okay to me."

"Boyfriends it is then." Ryan grinned and Johnny grinned back. *Damn.* Ryan really wanted to kiss him again but not here. Not with an audience. Because he had a feeling that once he started he wouldn't want to stop this time. "Wanna head back to your place… or mine?"

"Mine. Unless you have lube?"

James snorted and choked on his beer. "Oh my God, too much information."

Colin was still staring in amazement. "Well fuck." Ryan had obviously blown his mind.

Ryan picked up his drink. He had half a pint left and didn't want to waste it. "Want any?" He offered it to Johnny, who shook his head. So Ryan downed it and put the glass back down. "Sorry to ditch you, lads. Have a nice night."

"You too, you dirty bastard," James said, offering Ryan a fist to bump. "Take care guys, and congrats. I'm happy for you."

Out in the street, Ryan took Johnny's hand again. "This okay?" he asked.

"Yeah. If it's okay with you."

It was dark now, and although it felt strange walking along holding another man's hand, the street was quiet, and Ryan didn't think they'd attract any unwanted attention. He liked the feeling of Johnny's hand in his. "Yeah. It's good."

"That went well, the conversation with your mates," Johnny commented as they started to walk.

"I knew they'd be okay. James knew about you anyway, so it wasn't much of surprise for him. But Colin's cool too."

"What about the girls in your house? Are you okay with them knowing about us?"

"Yes. I'm fine with it. Bit anxious I guess, but I want to start telling people." Ryan couldn't deny he was nervous about coming out to more people. Not because he was worried about negative reactions from people he knew, but because once he started coming out as bisexual and telling people he was in a relationship with a guy, it would inevitably change people's perceptions of him. Word had a habit of spreading. His friends might be supportive, but wider acquaintances may be less so. *Fuck it.* Johnny was worth it. "I guess I'll need to tell my family too."

"There's no rush." Johnny squeezed his hand. "You can tell people at your own pace. Don't do it for me. It's only early days after all."

"We've been seeing each other a few weeks. We're together now, and I'm committed to giving it a go." Ryan stopped in his tracks and pulled Johnny to face him. He looked beautiful in the dim orange streetlights, eyes dark, and features chiselled. "You're my boyfriend. If you were a girlfriend, I'd mention it to my parents. So I want to tell them."

Johnny's smile was so sweet Ryan had to kiss him there and then, and Johnny kissed him back, deep and sure.

EIGHTEEN

Ryan was hungry for more kisses when they got back to the house. They went straight up to Johnny's room, bypassing the sound of his housemates in the living room. Johnny seemed to feel the same desperation, pressing Ryan up against the door as soon as it was shut behind them. He fumbled for the lock, flipping it with one hand as he groped Ryan's dick with the other.

"Fuck," Ryan muttered as Johnny rubbed him through his jeans. "I missed this. I missed *you*." He kissed Johnny again fiercely.

"I missed you too." Johnny pulled him in the direction of the bed. They hadn't put the light on, and they stumbled over something in the darkness. Johnny fell back on the bed with Ryan on top of him.

They kissed again, then Johnny pushed Ryan away. "Let me put the lamp on. And maybe get our shoes off."

Ryan rolled away to lie on his back and kicked off his trainers while Johnny fumbled around in the dark. There was a click, and the room was flooded with soft, warm light. Ryan looked up to see Johnny standing over him, eyes dark, and hair a chaotic mess. His T-shirt was hanging off one shoulder, collarbone exposed, and the bulge in his skinny jeans showed he was as turned on as Ryan.

"Get your clothes off," Ryan said, standing and taking off his own shirt.

They stripped quickly, then Ryan turned down the duvet and they got into bed, cool cotton on warm skin. Johnny pulled the covers up over them as they kissed, hands roaming and groping, stroking each other's torsos, squeezing hard cocks and firm arses. Johnny wriggled down under the covers to suck Ryan's cock and Ryan groaned as wet heat engulfed him. He pushed the duvet down. "I want to see you."

Johnny flicked his gaze up to meet Ryan's and tongued around the head, grinning seductively while Ryan tugged gently on his hair. He slid a hand around to grab Ryan's arse cheek—easy access as they were lying on their sides—and slid his fingers deliberately down Ryan's crack as he sucked him deep. Ryan gasped, lifting his upper leg to give Johnny better access, rewarded when those questing fingertips stroked over his hole. "Yeah," he muttered. "Feels good."

Nerve endings sparked as Johnny rubbed lightly, teasing and ticklish, while he sucked Ryan's cock harder. It was amazing, but only made Ryan want more. He grabbed Johnny's wrist and pulled his hand up. He kissed his fingertips and then drew them into his mouth, swirling his tongue around them until they were good and wet. Then he moved Johnny's hand back down to his arse and spread his legs wider in clear invitation.

Their gazes locked as Johnny pushed one finger slowly and deliberately into Ryan's hole. The sensation stole Ryan's breath and he tensed for a moment.

"Okay?" Johnny drew off to check.

"Yeah. It's good, just be gentle at first."

Smiling, Johnny went back to sucking him as he gradually began to move his finger in a slow, careful thrust.

Soon Ryan couldn't hold back his moans. Getting close, he was going to let Johnny make him come like this. He could fuck Johnny later, he was pretty sure they had all night because he wasn't leaving unless Johnny threw him out. But then the sound of footsteps on the stairs and the slam of the bathroom door distracted him and reminded him they weren't alone in the house. "Can you put some music on?" he asked.

"Sure." Johnny let his finger slip free and wiped it on the sheet before getting out of bed. He bent to pick up his jeans and retrieve his phone from the pocket, and Ryan gave an elaborate sigh.

"What?" Johnny asked innocently, looking over his shoulder with a knowing grin.

"That arse."

"Yours isn't so bad either." Johnny unlocked his phone, and then frowned as he looked at his screen. He hesitated for a moment, then sat down beside Ryan. "I don't need this anymore, do I?" His finger hovered over an icon Ryan didn't recognise, but that said Grindr underneath it.

Ryan put his hand on Johnny's thigh and squeezed. "I hope not."

As Ryan watched, Johnny deleted the app, then turned to him with a smile. "Gone. Now, what music do you want?"

"Anything chilled. Just some background noise to drown us out."

"You gonna be loud?"

"Probably. If you carry on doing what you were doing. It seems having things in my arse makes me noisy."

Johnny smirked. "Yeah. I remember. And that's just my fingers. God knows what you'd sound like with something bigger inside you." He got up again and put his phone on the docking station. Music began to play, slow but with a steady beat. Ryan remembered how amazing it had felt when Johnny had fingered him before. How different would his cock feel? The idea of it grew in Ryan's mind, trepidation mixed with want. But he trusted Johnny. He'd already trusted him with his body, and now he trusted him with his heart.

"I want you to fuck me," he said quickly.

Johnny's eyes widened, and a smile spread over his face. "Yeah? You sure?" He lay back down beside Ryan, searching his face as if for doubt.

"Very sure. As long as you want to do it too. You don't mind topping?"

"Not at all. I do love being fucked though, as you know. So if you turn into a greedy bottom who never wants to top me again then we might have a problem. But I'm happy to switch things up."

Ryan chuckled. "I don't think I'll ever want to give up topping, but I want to know how it feels to be fucked."

"Given how much you enjoyed being fingered, I think you're gonna love it."

Johnny kissed him, rolling on top of him and grinding down until they were both hard again. Something had shifted with Ryan asking Johnny to fuck him, and Johnny was more dominant than Ryan had ever known him. His kisses were demanding, his touch sure. Ryan responded instinctively by being more pliant. He yielded where normally he might resist or push back. He allowed Johnny to roll him over and push his legs apart, and when Johnny pulled up on his hips, he complied. Giving himself up to

Johnny was a strange, heady freedom. He got his knees under himself to push his arse up, open, and exposed while Johnny knelt behind him, hands on Ryan's hips.

"God you look good." Johnny's voice was rough with desire. "I can't believe I'm going to get to fuck you." He slid his palms over Ryan's buttocks, his thumbs gliding inwards. Then Ryan felt the tickle of warm breath. "Can I lick your arse?"

"Yeah," Ryan managed on a sigh, pushing back in invitation.

He was rewarded by the warm, wet touch of Johnny's tongue. Soft and ticklish, it was the best kind of torture. Not quite enough stimulation to push him to the edge, but enough to drive him crazy. Coupled with the mindfuck of being so vulnerable, of letting Johnny have access to his body this way, Ryan was soon drifting in a haze of arousal that felt almost unreal. The sensation changed, becoming more intense, and Ryan realised Johnny was using his fingers again.

"Just going to get the lube," Johnny said quietly and then Ryan was left hanging for a moment, empty and feeling the loss of contact. But then Johnny was there again, stroking his back, and pressing up close behind him to kiss Ryan's shoulders. "Still sure you want my cock in you?"

"Yes." Ryan had never been surer of anything.

"Okay. Jerk yourself off for me while I get a condom on."

Weirdly Ryan had almost forgotten about his dick when all the focus had been on his arse. But as soon as he started to stroke, it stiffened in his hand, ramping his desperation up another notch. He heard the sound of a condom wrapper, and the squirt of lube. Then Johnny's fingers were back, pushing easily into Ryan's hole. It felt tight, but so good, and Ryan gripped his dick, thumbing precome over the head as he moaned. "Yeah. Oh fuck. I want your cock."

"Where do you want it?" Johnny asked, slowly fucking his fingers in and out of Ryan in a way that made it almost impossible to concentrate on anything else.

"In my arse," Ryan gasped.

In one swift movement Johnny withdrew his fingers and replaced them with something bigger and smoother, blunt pressure rather than the sharper penetration of a fingertip. "Push back," Johnny gripped Ryan's hips. "Take it."

Ryan obeyed, easing back onto Johnny's cock until the head breached him and the stretch of it made him freeze, panting. It was definitely bigger than Johnny's fingers. For a moment, Ryan questioned whether this was a good idea. What if he couldn't do it? He'd ruin the mood if they had to stop, and he'd been so determined, so sure this was what he wanted.

"It's okay." Johnny held still, and ran his hands over the tense muscles in Ryan's back. "It should feel better soon, but we can stop if you want."

"No," Ryan bit out. "Gimme a minute."

"Stroke your cock again."

Ryan had softened with the discomfort, so he squeezed and stroked, getting himself hard again. By the time his erection was back, the burning stretch had subsided. He pushed back a little more, focusing on the pleasure of his hand on his cock and ignoring the ache in his arse, trusting it wouldn't last too long.

"Oh God," Johnny muttered. "Yeah, you've taken it all now." He gripped Ryan's hips again, pulling him back, but there was nowhere left to go.

Ryan squeezed around him and then released, and with that the last of his discomfort melted away. He felt full, overwhelmed, owned, but everything about it was good. "Fuck me."

Starting slowly, Johnny eased in and out. But soon Ryan was moving with him, encouraging him to go faster and harder by meeting his thrusts. It was primal, animalistic almost. Lost in the physical sensation of being fucked while he jerked himself off, Ryan had no room left in his head for self-consciousness or shame. Even if the music hadn't been playing there was no way he'd have been able to help the groans that Johnny knocked out of him as he hit Ryan's prostate with each deep slide of his cock.

"You close?" Johnny gritted out. "Because I am. Might need a breather if you're not gonna get there soon."

Ryan stroked his cock more insistently, rubbing it just right in a way that never failed. "Yeah. Nearly there." Johnny fucked him even harder and Ryan sped up the movement of his hand, giving into the pleasure as it built, blocks stacking up and up until they teetered and tumbled, and Ryan's climax crashed through him. "Oh fuck!" he cried out as his body jerked, come shooting out onto the bed beneath him in a series of pulses that seemed as if they'd never end.

"*Yes*," Johnny groaned, hips stilling, and Ryan felt the flex of his cock deep inside as he came too.

Legs shaking now, Ryan let his knees slide till he was flat on the bed and Johnny went with him, chuckling, and covering Ryan's body with his. He kissed Ryan's shoulders and stroked his head, tangling his fingers idly in Ryan's hair until his cock began to soften and slip free. The sensation of it sliding out with the condom still attached was ticklish and weird.

Ryan was still too exhausted to move, even though he was lying in a pool of come. He drifted in a dreamlike state as Johnny got rid of the condom and came back to the bed with a handful of tissues. "Want to clean up a bit?"

"I guess." Ryan heaved himself up and wiped his dick and his lubey arse, then dabbed ineffectually at the wet patch on the sheet. "Eh. It'll dry soon enough."

"Are you going to stay here tonight?" Johnny asked.

"Yes please. I should probably go back next door and get my toothbrush, but I can't be arsed."

"You can borrow mine."

"Thanks." Ryan smiled.

NINETEEN

Johnny woke to the sound of an unfamiliar ring tone. Sleepy and confused, it took him a moment to register why. There was a warm body snuggled up behind him and a heavy arm thrown over his waist, holding him close.

A smile spread over Johnny's face.

Ryan.

The ringing had stopped, but it started again a few minutes later. This time Johnny twisted around in Ryan's arms and patted his cheek. "Hey, your phone's ringing. Wanna see if it's important?"

"Huh?" Ryan cranked his eyes open and blinked sleepily. "Oh yeah. I suppose." He heaved himself out of bed and found his phone in his jeans from last night. The ringing had already stopped again, so he lay back down and squinted at the screen. "My mum," he said. "And then voicemail—probably from her. Guess I'd better listen to it."

He pressed a few buttons and Johnny could hear the tinny sound of a voice but couldn't pick out the words. He shuffled closer, stroking Ryan's chest, and admiring his profile. The scent of sex and come surrounded them. They'd woken in the middle of the night and fucked again—Ryan topping that time—so the bed was doused in both their jizz this morning. It should probably be gross, but Johnny kind of liked it.

"Everything okay?" he asked as Ryan took his phone away from his ear and ended the call.

"Yeah, she was just phoning to find out how my last couple of exams went. I forgot to text my parents yesterday with an update. I'll call her back later."

"You can do it now if you want? I don't mind. I can go and make us some coffee if you want privacy."

"No, it's fine. Stay here while I talk to her." Ryan put his free arm around Johnny, drawing him closer. Johnny lay his head on Ryan's shoulder and slid his arm around his torso to hold him tight. He loved being in Ryan's arms.

"Hi, Mum.... Yeah, no. I'm fine.... Sorry I forgot to text last night. I went out to celebrate, you know how it is.... Yes the exams went fine. I think I did the best I could, which is all I can do.... Mid-July I'll find out. So, how are things with you and Dad?"

There was a longer pause, and Ryan dipped his head to press a kiss to the top of Johnny's head while his mum was talking.

Johnny's heart did a little flip and he pressed an answering kiss to Ryan's chest, just above his nipple.

Ryan was mostly listening now, interjecting with the occasional, "Mmm," or "That's good," or a chuckle at some bit of news his mum was sharing.

"Yeah it was good to catch up, Mum. I'm glad all is well with you. Actually, before you go"—Ryan's arm tightened around Johnny's shoulders—"I have a bit of news myself.

I've started seeing someone and I wanted to tell you about them." Johnny stiffened at the pronoun. Was Ryan going to be evasive? He'd almost rather not be mentioned at all if that was the case. But he was quickly reassured by Ryan's next words. "Actually, it's a he, Mum."

There was a pause while that bit of information was digested. Then Ryan's mum said something else, and damn, Johnny wished he could hear both sides of the conversation. He drew back so he could see Ryan's face. Ryan glanced sideways, expression anxious, and his jaw tense.

Please let her be cool. Johnny's heart pounded hard and every muscle in his body was drawn tight.

Ryan chuckled nervously. "Yeah, it was a surprise for me too.... No, Mum, it doesn't mean I'm gay now. I'm pretty sure I'm bisexual actually. But the important part is that Johnny—that's his name—is awesome, and I really like him a lot. I think you and Dad will too.... Yes, hopefully you'll get a chance to meet him fairly soon.... Okay, I'll ask him.... Yes, he's here with me now. Hang on."

Ryan covered his phone with his hand and turned to Johnny. "I was planning on going back to visit them for a few days at the end of July, before I start work. Would you come with me? Assuming that everything is going well between us then?"

The idea of being introduced to Ryan's parents was scary as hell, but it was also amazing. And if Ryan wanted him to meet the family then Johnny was game. He grinned, stomach flipping with nerves and excitement. "Yes. I'd love to."

Ryan leaned over and kissed him, quick and soft, before drawing back to say, "He said yes.... Okay, Mum, I'd better go. Send my love to Dad and I'll call again soon... or sure, we can FaceTime when Dad's around too.... Bye.... Love you too."

He ended the call and put his phone down on the floor before rolling back to Johnny.

"Well, that seemed to go okay." Johnny couldn't wipe the smile off his face, but there was one on Ryan's that matched it.

"Yeah. My parents are cool. I knew it would be a surprise, but not a bad one. And they've got a few weeks to get used to the idea before they meet you."

"And it gives me time to plan what to wear. I want to look my best to meet your parents, make a good impression. I'm not sure my black skinny jeans and boots will cut it. And I should probably ditch the eyeliner."

"No way. You look hot like that. And my parents won't judge. Seriously. You should see the old photos of what they used to wear in the eighties. My dad used to wear ruffles and velvet and shit like that—and more eyeliner than you ever do."

Johnny laughed. "Wow. That's awesome. I demand to see those photos when I visit."

"Deal."

Ryan rolled Johnny over onto his back and gazed down at him. The playful humour was gone, replaced by intensity. His expression was full of desire, but something softer too, something that made Johnny's heart swell as well as quicken. Emotion rushed through him and a feeling of connection so strong it was overwhelming. "Kiss me," he said, afraid of what he might say if his mouth wasn't occupied.

When their lips met it was a different form of communication, and so was Ryan's hand cupping Johnny's cheek, stroking him like he was something precious. It might be too early to use words to express how they felt about each other, but they showed each other through touch. Rolling onto their sides they took each other's cocks in hand, still kissing each other wherever they could reach—lips, cheeks, necks, and then locking their mouths together again as they got closer. Johnny came first, and Ryan followed after, moaning into the kiss as they stroked each other slowly through it.

"You need to buy more tissues," Ryan said as they mopped up.

"I think it's your turn to buy some. And condoms too."

"Yeah. Fair enough."

A knock on the door surprised them both.

"Yeah? Who is it?"

"It's Mac," a voice called. "We're making house breakfast downstairs. Eggs, bacon, sausages, beans.... The works. Do you want some?"

"Do you?" Johnny whispered to Ryan, who nodded and gave a thumbs up.

"Got enough for me plus one?" Johnny shouted back.

"Yep."

"In that case, yes please. We'll be down in a few."

AS THEY ENTERED the kitchen hand-in-hand, they were greeted by a chorus of whoops and claps. All of Johnny's housemates, plus Ewan, were there with huge shit-eating grins on their faces. The air was thick with the scent of cooking bacon and slightly burned toast.

"I take it you sorted things out then?" Ewan said to Ryan.

Ryan's grip tightened on Johnny's hand. "Yeah. We did."

"Awesome."

"Yeah, congrats guys." Jez gave them a thumbs up.

"Okay, I reckon this bacon is finally crispy enough," Shawn said from by the cooker. "Can we start getting stuff on plates now?"

They all hurried to do things, some hindering as much as helping as they got in each other's way trying to get out plates and cutlery, and get the food dished up before it got cold. There was a lot of noise and bickering, but somehow they finally got it all sorted.

They ate in the living room. Jez, Mac, Jude, and Shawn at the table; while Johnny and Ryan sat on one sofa, and Ewan and Dev on the other.

"God this is great," Ryan said. "Thanks so much guys. Can I contribute something towards the food?"

"There's no need," Mac said. "We quite often do a house breakfast on a weekend, and I assume you're going to be staying over more now, so you can bring something another time."

"Okay, cool." Ryan took another forkful of scrambled eggs.

Forgetting his food for a moment, Johnny looked around him. Jez and Mac's feet were tangled together under the table. Shawn and Jude were eating one-handed, their free hands clasped together on the tabletop. Ewan and Dev were swapping food to and from each other's plates, Dev taking Ewan's sausage and giving him his bacon in return. Those little signs of casual intimacy no longer made Johnny feel envious like they had recently. Now they made him happy, because he could have that too.

He shuffled a little closer to Ryan and let his knee drop sideways so they were pressed together.

"You okay?" Ryan asked through a mouthful of food, turning to look at him.

Johnny grinned, and put his fork down so he could catch a stray bit of baked bean juice on Ryan's lip with his fingertip. "Yeah. I'm awesome."

EPILOGUE

"This is where we get off," Ryan said as the train started to slow.

The rhythm of the wheels on the tracks altered as the greens and browns of the countryside outside the train window changed to more urban colours: the white and brick-red of houses, and the grey of stone walls and streets.

Johnny stood, swaying with the motion of the carriage as he began to make his way down the centre aisle with Ryan following behind. He admired Johnny's arse, as always. Habit drew his gaze there whenever he had the opportunity to look. He'd tried to talk Johnny out of wearing his ubiquitous black skinny jeans and boots due to the oppressive July heat, but now he was glad he'd failed. They showcased Johnny's butt like nothing else did.

They collected their rucksacks from the luggage rack. Ryan's blue and relatively new, compared to Johnny's ancient battered black one. Ryan's was also much less full than Johnny's, which was almost bursting at the seams. He'd spent ages dithering over which clothes to pack, worrying about impressing Ryan's parents, and had ended up packing what looked like half his wardrobe to keep his options open.

As the train finally shuddered to a halt, Ryan was the first off, waiting for Johnny on the platform so they could walk side-by-side. There was nobody checking tickets at the small country station, so they walked through the open gate to the car park and out onto the street beyond. On the edge of the small commuter town where Ryan had been brought up, the road to the station was lined by grassy banks, thick with wild flowers, and overhung by trees.

"How far is it to your parents' house?" Johnny asked.

"Not very far. It will take us about ten minutes, maybe less if we walk fast."

"Can I vote for walking slowly?"

Ryan grinned. "Because of the heat, or because you're nervous? Wouldn't it be better to get it over with now?"

"Both. But I'll be more confident about meeting them if I'm not a sweaty mess." Johnny tucked a flyaway strand of hair behind his ear.

"Okay," Ryan said. But the chances of not being a sweaty mess were slim to none. The heat of his rucksack was already making his T-shirt stick to his back, and Johnny had damp patches beginning to form at the armpits of his new hot-pink T-shirt. "You look gorgeous though, babe. Seriously."

Johnny glanced sideways with a cheeky smile. "You're biased. You always think I look gorgeous."

"Because you are."

Ryan stopped and grabbed Johnny's hand. He tugged him gently around and cupped his cheek. Flushed from the heat with the barest sprinkling of summer freckles on his nose, Johnny was even more stunning than usual. His blond hair was bright in the sunlight, which lit his grey eyes as though from within. The usual dark smudge of eyeliner emphasised them. Ryan had been very insistent that Johnny didn't need to change his appearance for meeting his family. He wanted them to see the real Johnny in all his quirky glory, not some faux-conventional version.

"You're staring at me." Johnny's lips quirked.

"Because you're so pretty. I can't help it." Ryan leaned closer and pressed his mouth to Johnny's. Johnny kissed him back, and Ryan put his hands on Johnny's hips and pulled him even closer. He moved one hand to the small of Johnny's back and let his fingers dip beneath Johnny's waistband. Feeling something with his fingertips that caught his attention, he dipped a little lower and groaned.

"Seriously?" He drew back to see Johnny smiling wickedly. "You're wearing lace. Today? What happened to trying to be 'normal' for my parents—your words, not mine."

"Your parents aren't going to see my underwear," Johnny said with a shrug. "It makes me feel more... I don't know. Confident around new people sometimes. Like I have a secret that they don't know. They might judge me on what they can see, but they can't see everything."

"Is it the pink ones?" Ryan asked.

Johnny nodded, grin widening.

"Damn, Johnny. Knowing you're wearing those isn't going to make *me* feel more comfortable. You know that just the thought of them is enough to make me distracted."

"Well, we can be uncomfortable together then."

"And I won't even be able to fuck you later because you refused to pack any lube," Ryan grumbled.

"Ry, we've been through this. We're not fucking in your parents' house. It's way too messy even with condoms, and neither of us are capable of being quiet enough when we bottom."

"Blowjobs are okay though, right?"

Johnny chuckled. "Blowjobs are fine. No mess."

Ryan kissed him again, reaching his hand even further down the back of Johnny's jeans until the sound of a car approaching made them jump apart and move quickly to the side of the narrow lane.

"Right." Johnny adjusted his dick and tugged his jeans up at the back where Ryan had shoved them down a little. "Let's go and introduce me to your parents."

SITTING AWKWARDLY on the sofa with Johnny, Ryan was reminded of the first time he'd brought a girlfriend home. He'd been fourteen at the time and his mum had insisted on making tea and feeding them biscuits. His parents had both tried to make polite conversation with the girl while Ryan just wanted them to sod off and leave them in peace.

Now, though, he was grateful for his mum and dad's efforts to make Johnny feel welcome. The biscuits had been upgraded to carrot cake, but the tea was the same—in the best cups and saucers, and out of a pot—and so was the polite conversation.

"I wasn't planning on staying in retail, but as the assistant manager position came up, I thought I'd go for it," Johnny was saying. "I'm enjoying the extra responsibility, and might stay with the company if there is a chance I can advance more. I'm also interested in getting more into the marketing side of things. That would be a more nine-to-five job, which would be nice. Then my hours would be more in line with Ryan's." Johnny glanced sideways at Ryan and smiled affectionately.

Ryan smiled back, cheeks flushing. "That would be great."

It felt weird to be sitting close but not touching. Normally they were very tactile, but Ryan wasn't sure how Johnny would feel if Ryan tried to hold his hand or touch his knee in front of his parents. He kept his hands to himself for now. Hopefully once they were all a bit more relaxed and less formal it would feel more natural to reach for him.

"Yes, I remember it was hard when your father worked weekend and evening shifts. It's definitely easier to have quality time together if your schedules mesh," Ryan's mum said.

His dad chuckled. "Especially when the kids were small. Quality time was almost non-existent. Although I suppose that won't be a problem for you two."

Johnny stiffened, and Ryan floundered, unsure how to respond.

"That's not true at all, dear," his mum chipped in. "Lots of same-sex couples have children these days—not that I'm putting pressure on you for grandchildren," she added to Ryan and Johnny. "But that's a very outdated assumption, so I wanted to set your father strai—" She stopped, flushing bright pink and then changing tack. "I wanted to correct him."

Johnny made a strange snorting noise and covered it with a cough.

Changing the subject Ryan said desperately, "How's Connie? Is she going to be coming over this weekend at all?" Connie was his older sister who lived quite locally with her boyfriend.

"Yes," Ryan's dad replied. "She's coming for lunch tomorrow with Miles. And she's very well, a bit fed up with her current job but is applying for new ones and has a few interviews coming up."

The awkward moment passed as the conversation moved on.

When they'd finished their tea and cake, Ryan's mum started to gather up the plates.

"Let me help, Mum," Ryan offered.

Johnny seemed fine, deep in conversation with Ryan's dad about music. They'd just got onto eighties bands, and Ryan's dad was in his element.

Ryan gathered up the plates while his mum put the cups and saucers back on the tea tray. He followed her through to the kitchen and put them down by the sink.

"Oh, Ryan," his mum said in a hushed tone. "I'm so sorry for putting my foot in it. What an idiot."

"Mum, it's fine. The word straight isn't offensive you know. We wouldn't have even noticed if you hadn't made a big deal out of it."

"I know. I'm just trying so hard to get things right, and then I messed up."

"Stop worrying. The only way you could get things not right would be if you had a problem with me and Johnny being a couple, and you don't, right?"

"Of *course* not!" She looked horrified at the mere thought.

"So chill out, and stop trying so hard. Okay?"

"Okay." She nodded. Then she looked at Ryan intently. "I can see how much you care about him, it's obvious when you look at him."

"Yeah," Ryan admitted. "I care about him a lot."

"And he's a lovely-looking boy—well, man really I suppose—incredibly pretty, especially in that pink T-shirt which looks gorgeous on him." She faltered again. "Is it wrong to say he's pretty? Handsome is better I suppose."

"Johnny doesn't mind being called pretty," Ryan assured her. "He'd take it as a compliment, believe me."

"Well good, because he is pretty. But the most important thing is that he's making my boy happy." She smiled. "Isn't he?"

"Yes, Mum." Ryan paused, joy swelling his chest as he heard the sound of Johnny's muffled voice in the living room, and his dad's answering peal of laughter. "He really is."

ABOUT THE AUTHOR

Jay lives just outside Bristol in the West of England. He comes from a family of writers, but always used to believe that the gene for fiction writing had passed him by. He spent years only ever writing emails, articles, or website content.
One day, Jay decided to try and write a short story—just to see if he could—and found it rather addictive. He hasn't stopped writing since.

Jay is transgender and was formerly known as she/her.

www.jaynorthcote.com
Twitter: @Jay_Northcote
Facebook: Jay Northcote Fiction

MORE FROM JAY NORTHCOTE

The Housemates Series

Helping Hand – Housemates #1
Like a Lover – Housemates #2
Practice Makes Perfect – Housemates #3
Watching and Wanting – Housemates #4
Starting from Scratch – Housemates #5

Other Novels and Novellas

Nothing Serious
Nothing Special
Nothing Ventured
Not Just Friends
Passing Through
The Little Things
The Dating Game – Owen & Nathan #1
The Marrying Kind – Owen & Nathan #2

The Law of Attraction
Imperfect Harmony
Into You
Cold Feet
What Happens at Christmas
A Family for Christmas
Summer Heat
Tops Down Bottoms Up
The Half Wolf
Secret Santa

ACKNOWLEDGEMENTS

Thank you my editor Victoria Milne, for making my words better; my alpha reader Lennan Adams for keeping me going and not letting me give up; and my proof readers: Annabelle Jacobs, Jen, Justyna, N.R. Walker, and Rita. And last but never least—thank you to all my readers for supporting me and reminding me on a daily basis why I write.

Made in the USA
Columbia, SC
26 February 2018